KM Beirne

The Unfortunate Ones

Prelude

"Blood Dreams," Vita slowly nodded knowingly, her small, plain face full of absolute seriousness as she stared knowingly into the wide, bright, emerald eyes of her drinking companion, "that's how they pass on their knowledge and their memories to the other members of their tribe so that nothing is ever lost to them as a people. When one Decona perishes, their blood is drained by the others and each tribe member will consume some of it before going to sleep that night. Then, in the depths of slumber, their dreams will uncover to them everything that the deceased Decona ever knew or learnt...and they will never forget that knowledge, and when it is their turn to depart this life the same thing will happen to them. If they cannot drain the body of one of their own, then the precious memories and knowledge are lost forever and so they will fight just as voraciously with claws and teeth to protect their dead as they will to protect their living. The Decona would mourn deeply for any of their kind to be taken from them and never returned."

Vita's expression had taken on a wistful look as she became engrossed in her own story-telling and she had not noticed the tendrils of wispy brown hair that had fallen around her eyes as her head had nodded along with her words.

Everhart smoothed his uneven beard downwards with a graceful stroke of his right hand, despite its immense size. The beard itched abominably, but he liked to think that it made him look older and wiser, not to mention more dashing and so it remained, although its maintenance was a bit lackadaisical to say the least, often shorn unevenly in haste. Everhart Bovenwater abhorred people thinking he was young and inexperienced and often felt as if he had to prove his worth to the world. Helplessness was not a characteristic that he liked or tolerated being attributed to him.

"You know my dear Vita, if you didn't have such a peculiar way of being right all the time, I'd swear you were pulling my leg. Pull the other leg if you like, it has wind chimes on! Blood Dreams...Decona...all myth and legend if you ask me. But, I never did like to call you wrong" he smiled jovially, directing a playful wink at his companion and then rose from the old, worn, wooden bar-stool, cracking his muscles leisurely before turning to leave the dank tavern that was the only choice for a drink and a bit of banter in the secluded village of Aither.

It took less than a moment for Vita to snap out of her self-induced musing.

"No more myth and legend than that damn soothsaying feline of yours Everhart!" Vita hissed under her breathe angrily at Everhart's colossal shoulders, her delicate hands placed firmly upon her slender hips indicating her annoyance perfectly, whilst her slight nostrils flared in defiance of behaving appropriately. She was acutely aware that Everhart had not intended to offend her but whenever she was questioned or disbelieved it irked her temper irrationally and it was too late now anyway, for she had already broached Everhart's most sensitive topic.

The intimidating muscle and height of Everhart did not impede his quickness in the slightest as he whirled around and clamped his meaty fist over Vita's thin, wrist. He pulled her close to his wide chest, firmly but not aggressively and bent down to her ear.

"You know not to mention him in this place woman! One word of him to the wrong people and he'll be hunted down like prey and imprisoned, tortured and..." He let out a sorrowful, heart-wrenching sigh and released Vita's pale, bony wrist dejectedly. "He's everything to me Vita, everything - my truest friend. I made a solemn promise to him all those years ago that I would never let them get to him. He doesn't deserve this danger forever looming over him, he's no danger to anyone Vita, and damn he doesn't even eat meat! He isn't even a danger to those damn squawking chickens that run around Aither! They are more likely to cause a death or injury the way that they get under your feet all the time. There is far too much talk of myth and legend brewing of late, and it isn't so readily dismissed as it used to be, which puts him in even more danger than ever before! I've spent all these years trying to protect him...keeping him a secret from people...but I fear I've kept him too close to civilization…if you can call Aither that."

Everhart rolled his eyes, his anger now completely extinguished as he spoke softly to Vita.

"You figured it out yourself with no evidence at all didn't you? I mean, I know you are brighter than most but still... Please Vita; help me get him away from Aither and away from people. I can feel evil brewing, even here, can't you?"

Everhart's sudden dramatic change from teasing and playful to furious and then pleading revealed to Vita the stark depth of his fear and plainly revealed it as a long-grown, deep-rooted emotion. Rubbing her wrist thoughtfully where Everhart's hand had grasped it but a moment before, Vita nodded her head slowly, her own anger evaporating like spilt water on a scorching summer afternoon, when seeing her own friend's genuine distress and fear.

"I'm truly sorry Ever, you know my temper snaps and I am quick to bite when people won't understand me. Come on, I agree with you that trouble is brewing - I feel it in my bones. I even heard old Barley banging on about ghosts and ghouls last week when I went to get my bread, and you of all people now how sceptical he is of anything. I fear even the outskirts of an inferior village like Aither isn't secluded enough for him anymore. You have been a true friend to him and also to me when I have had need and you truly have done well to keep his existence unknown here for all this time, but, yes, I feel it too. Let's get him out then. Tonight will not be soon enough and truly I don't need much time to get what little things that I have together."

Everhart nodded thankfully. Vita's calm assumption that she would be accompanying him also brooked no room for argument and made him feel relieved and slightly irritated at the same time. However, he tried his best to conceal his mixed emotions and retain his composure and manners and scooping up Vita's forest green, winter cloak and floating it around her slight shoulders, he set a protective arm there too before heading off with his companion to make provisions for the unknown journey ahead.

As the two friends headed purposefully toward the hazy light of the splintered tavern door, they were too engrossed in their own thoughts and worries to notice the shabbily dressed figure who had sat alone in the darkness of the tavern corner tilt his worn hat to follow their departure. Nor had they noticed that he had never taken his eyes off them throughout the entirety of their hushed conversation.

1

The lush, rich, leafy undergrowth of Aither's surrounding forest land smelt heavy yet also fresh, earthy and untainted to Everhart's keen nose. This haven of unblemished nature was his true home, not the noisy, humid bakery back in Aither's dusty village. Aither's untroubled forest had been his favoured place to escape to when he was helpless and young as a boy, running from the floury backhanded cuffs of the impatient baker that had grudgingly taken him in when his loving parents had failed to return from the expedition to the soothsayer's enchanted lands. The thick, curved boughs of the welcoming trees had never denied him refuge, had never judged him or turned him away when he had wearily clambered into their embrace to weep silently into his scuffed, pulled up knees. The enchanting forest treetop had also been where he had met him for the first time, also weeping, also mournfully alone in the world.

The powerful blow came from behind, suddenly and unexpectedly as Everhart had wandered thoughtfully through ancient memories, joyous and melancholy, unprepared for such an unprovoked attack. His breath was knocked from him harshly as he was rolled roughly onto his back by the adept predator.

"Loki you colossal lummox!" rasped Everhart half-seriously, irritated to have still been taken by surprise after all these years, rolling out from underneath the massive tiger and diving on his thick neck to knuckle the feline's head.

"Bloody be careful would you!" The worry and anxiety dissolved as quickly as it had serviced as Everhart playfully wrestled with the big cat, pure happiness welling up inside him to know that his friend was still protected - still safe and unharmed by the jealous, paranoid touch of humans.

The tiger was more experienced at play-fighting now, careful not to let his deathly talons rake Ever's curly-haired arms enough to draw blood, unlike when they were both cubs together in years gone by. When Everhart was finally out of breath from the raucous wrestling, Loki sat back on his powerful haunches and began to systematically clean the inky, black pads of his paws with shiny, curved fangs, careful not to push Everhart too far from playfulness to irritability.

"Loki, my dear friend, there is something of the utmost importance that I need to tell...to discuss with you" began Everhart hesitantly when he had recovered his breath and dusted himself off, kneeling down on the leaf-strewn forest floor in front of the admirable tiger and resting one calloused hand on the warm, soft fur of his muscly shoulders whilst he nervously brushed forest debris from his green breeches. He breathed in slowly as he thought about where to begin, how to tell his closest friend that he was about to drag him away from the place where they had grown up together, from the only place he had known since childhood.

The tiger nudged Everhart's arm with his wedge-shaped head and flipped his hand up to scratch behind his rounded ears with a cold, wet nose.

"Well of course I know all that already Ever," he purred warmly and smugly, as he tilted his head to the right to encourage Everhart's fingers to move to a particularly itchy spot. "I'm still a soothsayer you know. How long is Vita going to be with that food by the way? Honestly, you'd think the girl would be a bit quicker by now at filching a few loafs of bread and wedges of cheese from miserable old Barley! The man's old enough that a sloth could outfox him on a particularly sleepy day."

A relieved smirk found its way onto Everhart's face as his hands slipped onto his waist in a parody of Vita's angry stance. "Well damn me if I let that small detail slip my concerned mind. I didn't know you would be watching my thoughts you sneaky, striped devil. Don't trust me enough not to have a bit of fun without involving you, do you?"

"How many times do I have to tell you that it doesn't work that way you dense human," Loki gurgled back in a semblance of laughter, "this knowledge arrives unlooked for in my dreams, unfortunately I cannot pick and choose what I see, else I would know to avoid your whereabouts after you visit the tavern and reek of that odious poison you insist on swilling back." The tiger cocked his head to the right and wrinkled his whiskers upwards so it almost looked like he was grinning.

"You dreamt it!? When Loki? Exactly what did you dream? What's happening? Will we be alright?!" with every question Everhart's hands waved frantically as if he were swatting annoying mist flies away that were intent on suckling his blood.

"If you pause for a breath Everhart Bovenwater, then perhaps I could try to answer your unquenchable string of questions!" Loki growled softly, butting his head against Everhart's beard-covered chin. "Again, you know that it doesn't work like that my worrisome friend. I dream in ideas, thoughts and shapes, not in facts etched in lifeless rock in the order of the way that they will happen. The images come to me in slumber as they will with no concern for my wishes of how they should arrive, and I do my utmost to unravel what they all mean. All I know is that this afternoon a dark shadow began to take shape and grow in my dreams. It whipped itself up to a menacing size and gave chase to me through the undergrowth. Vita and you appeared beside me, haversacks of supplies bouncing on your shoulders as we ran together furiously, ran to a place of cold mountains and strangeness to escape the ever-growing shadow's pursuit and leave Aither behind."

The usual playful and relaxed nature of the great cat seem to have vanished as his serious emerald eyes that were so like

Everhart's himself, bore deeply into his soul, portraying a being burdened and vastly older than Loki's years or experience.

"I assumed that this meant that leaving was inevitable and close too, and I must be correct as here you are before me, my friend. Yet Vita is not and hence I surmise that she has snuck off to gain supplies for the journey, being as she is so much more agile than yourself you great oxen. You intended to break the news to me whilst you waited for her to catch up with enough food to get us a goodly distance from this place...no?"

A single nod was all that was needed between the two, both knew it would be painful to leave the beloved forest that held so many of their happy memories behind and yet both also knew that if a foretelling had occurred they had no choice in the matter if they wanted to avoid disaster. Like Vita, Loki was seldom wrong and Everhart was cautious enough not to chance ignoring the soothsayer.

Loki's ears swivelled backwards suddenly at the sound of a snapping twig broken in the undergrowth nearby and both he and Everhart rapidly whirled into crouching stances ready to fight the encroaching threat. Everhart's large hand curled around the worn blade of the knife at his hip whilst the striped fur on Loki's back and neck bristled upwards just as his black lips curled up to reveal a row of sharp, yellowed fangs.

Vita strolled merrily into the clearing with a slight skip in her step, lugging two tan, leather haversacks over each shoulder and raised an eyebrow and a corner of her thin lips curiously, "Planning on having me for lunch boys are you? Everhart led me to form an impression that you did not partake in meat Loki, however I confess I must have been mistaken as the pair of you look hungry and vicious enough to take down a charging herd of wild deer." Vita let the haversack's fall to the ground unafraid as she made a courtly bow to the tiger and then boldly held out her hand towards him in greeting.

The tiger and his constant defender relaxed their tense bodies and as Everhart exhaled in pure relief, Loki drew himself up and puffed out his expansive chest, "Oh quite to the contrary my dear, I abhor the consumption of flesh purely to satisfy needs that could easily be satisfied elsewhere, but if one will go tramping around the forest with all the grace of an intoxicated elephant then you must expect fugitives to be put ever slightly on edge."

Everhart grimaced and scrunched his eyes as he awaited one of Vita's famous outbursts for she was not one to be insulted, Loki had likely just blown their chances of aid from her in one fell swoop.

Her womanly, coy giggle brightened up the dense woods, "Indeed Master Loki. Perhaps I shall learn some elegance from your kind self on our travels together? Shall we be on our way then?" she asked as she silked his ears back with her proffered hand.

Loki bobbed his head, bowed graciously and allowed Vita to rest a slender arm upon his back as they strode off northwards in a companionable silence.

Confused, Everhart grabbed both haversacks from the ground where Vita had abandoned them before curtsying to Loki, and quickly hurried after them "Why in carnation hasn't that ever worked for me before!" he scowled. "Bloody woman! I swear I'll never understand them!"

2

"Bloody useless I tell you! Ever since he was a child. Took him in out of the kindness of my own heart I did and how does he repay me? By gallivanting off to the tavern every opportunity he gets. Well he won't be getting any supper here tonight! Even my patience and good-nature has an end!" Barley ranted as he kneaded the milky ball of dough furiously under his chubby palms ensuring flour puffed up chokingly into the eyes of his visitor.

"I can completely sympathise with you Master Wheatflour, it's enough to make one's heart break clear in two," Willian sighed emphatically giving a theatrical slow shake of his head, "why it was just yesterday that with my own eyes I witnessed the ungrateful sot drinking all your honest money away at the bar with some plain, tavern whore. I've no doubt a man of your intellect and observational skills witnessed the truth of my tale when Everhart stumbled in late last night, no?" Willian looked down at his hands and picked his slim nails feigning disinterest at Everhart's whereabouts and that the question was no more than mere courtesy.

An unamused snort escaped Barley's flabby throat, "last night? Last night he didn't even design to grace me with his presence at all. In fact I haven't seen the lazy cretin all morning or afternoon either! I expect he's passed out in an alley somewhere the lazy layabout! I've a good mind to turn him out completely you know," his tirade continued with much jabbing at the air with swollen, floury fingers "he's an adult now after all, I shouldn't have to make such sacrifices as I good-natured have since his parents left him here with me without a care for how I would cope." Barley had conveniently forgotten to mention the savings that Everhart's parents had given him to care for their only child and see that he was well taught and cared for whilst they were gone on a quest to learn more about the fate of their emerald eyed son.

The anxious look barely ornamented Willian's quaint features for a moment before he smoothed them away with a habit borne from much practice and replaced them with a pleasant, understanding smile. "I am sure people can see you have done all with him that you can Master Wheatflour. It pains me to see how your kindness is disregarded without a second thought." He shook his head again theatrically and signed as he waited just long enough so that it didn't seem odd or rude that he was leaving so soon after his arrival. "I'm afraid I have business to attend to now my good sir so I must leave but I will be certain to let you know if I make sight of Everhart. Have a good day sir." Willian doffed his old hat politely and strolled slowly out of the stuffy bakery, not hurrying until he was well out of sight.

Now, where would that troublesome trio likely to be headed? He had been sure that they would have made more preparations before they left Aither! Damn, why hadn't he followed Everhart and Vita the moment that they had left the tavern yesterday! He had been sure he would have had at least a few days before they fled. Aither's surrounding forest was where Everhart always seemed to be headed towards, although Willian had never caught sight of the beast that he was certain existed - certain that Everhart miserly kept all for himself! But he knew it was there - oh yes - he knew! He had spotted the flame coloured hairs that had often adorned Everhart's jerkin, heard the distant growls in the forest when Everhart was there and he had been taught the legends by his father of what power such a beast could grant! Then there were Everhart's suspicious parents. His father had told him all about them as well. All about their high and mighty expectations for their son with his emerald, soothsayer tainted eyes. Willian stalked back to his room at the tavern determinedly to gather some food and what meagre money he had left. He wrapped the food in an, old, torn handkerchief and bundled it into his wearing haversack hastily. Willian distributed his money between his haversack, pocket and boot before setting off to the forest to be sure that if he encountered a pickpocket then they didn't make off with all his money at once. Surely he could pick up some trace or clue when he reached that damned forest?

    Willian didn't have to carry out his expedition completely alone and desolate however. He decided that he would take 'the unfortunate' along with him. The child, if it could be called that, had been his for a little over a year now. At first, Willian had found the child-creature utterly revolting. The child was certainly not normal by any standards. Its age was completely impossible to determine but it stood about five foot and two inches from the ground. Willian only thought of it as a child in his head as it lacked almost all the qualities you would associate with an adult. Its skin was a deathly, pale, grey hue and as of a consistency more akin to cheap message paper than human skin. Long, matted white hair hung grimly from its scalp as far down as its waist. It's arms and legs didn't seem to have formed properly and seemed to be twisted in a distinctly unpleasant way, which led to it shuffling in a contorted, loping way whenever it walked. But for all those negativities, the creature did have its uses. It never spoke, not even a word, which was always a bonus in Willian's opinion. Willian wasn't sure if the creature did not have the capability to talk or it if was just a personal choice, but he didn't much care. Never one for sentiment, Willian hadn't deigned to name the child-creature, instead simply referring to him as 'the unfortunate', when he wasn't angry that is. When irritable he often referred to him as his freak on a leash as it was as if the creature was pulled along on an invisible lead, so attached to him was he.

    The Unfortunate had simply followed him back to the Inn one frosty night when there was no one else around and the streets were eerily quiet. Where it came from, Willian did not know, and even after much kicking and batting away, the unfortunate thing would not leave. Willian had ignored it for a few days but soon discovered that although it was mute, it communicated with him to a certain extent and was quite tractable and able to perform errands as required in exchange fora few scraps of the worst looking food that Willian had in his possession.

The dank, dark forest was cold and unwelcoming to Willian, as if it wanted to deny him entry and he wrinkled his nose at the damp stench that invaded his nostrils. Last night's downpour of rain gave an eerie glow to the dew-covered branches and leaves as they sparkled in the moonlight. Anyone who willingly spent time here must be up to something unclean and Willian had a duty to put a stop to it, he judiciously thought to himself as he studied the uneven ground around as he walked, whilst the unfortunate creature quietly trailed a few paces behind him.

Willian had thought the sodden earth would at least make it easier to track Everhart, his whore-friend and the un-natural beast, yet he found no trace of footprints in the muddy surroundings no matter how closely he examined the ground. Exasperated he hunched down under a bowed down branch and chewed on a stale crust of bread from his haversack as he pondered his next move. The Unfortunate ambled to sit in front of him as a chewed, staring at the bread longingly whilst a string of slobber began to drip from the corner of its cracked, grey lips. Disgusted, Willian tore a small chunk of crust from the edge and threw it to the dirty ground away from him in order for him to eat in peace and be able to think. The creature shuffled after it and stooped to the floor to retrieve it. It stuffed the bread into its mouth with no regard for the mud that still clung to it from the forest floor.

Willian tried to ignore the creature as he mused. He was sure his Father would have known what to do next if this golden opportunity had presented itself to him. He was a wise man who seemed to have a knack of knowing every legend there was. Whether it be soothsayers, gargoyles, dragons or Decona. The answer had to be amongst these things! Now to seek someone with access to more knowledge of these things and ensure they helped him whether they wanted to or not.

3

Vita rubbed her slender hands together briskly over the crackling fire to warm them through as she talked, "Well it'll be no good for us to stop and look for safety anywhere this side of the mountain Ever although I know you already know this is to be true. It would be too easy for someone to find us if they went looking. The only place to hide close to home was Aither's woodland and we've already left there. I'm telling you my friend that it is the only way we have left as an option. We must go through the distant mountain to get as far away as possible! I've heard that it comes right out on the other side with no need to travel over the treacherous top of the mountain, which I don't mind admitting that I would have a bit of difficulty in achieving."

"Oh yes, we'll just stroll right up to the front door of the neighbourly lizard men and ask if they wouldn't mind terribly guiding us on our way through their home if they have the time. And if they could avoid spearing us and roasting us for dinner before drinking our blood at the same time, then that would be extraordinarily decent of them!" Everhart stared at Vita angrily as he spouted his bitter reply and rubbed his temples wearily.

Vita drew a breath ready to bite back at Everhart's angry response but was interrupted before she had the chance.

"Do I get a say in this at all or is it down to you bickering two-legs?" yawned Loki lazily as he stretched his front legs downwards, his sharp talons gripping the earth for purchase to crack out his stiff muscles. "As if I did, I would say whilst it would be a bit unnerving stepping into the unknown, Vita's plan truly does appear to be our only option. Despite the gory tales that you may have had passed down to you around the village Everhart, I do not foresee the Decona causing any problems for us if we don't cause any problems for them. Their ways are peculiar to us, true, but let us not forget they drink the blood of their deceased only to pass on memories, not the blood of humans willy-nilly. I do not think this means that they consume each other whenever they feel like it or indeed that they feel they have to gorge on any creature's flesh that happens to wander by."

Everhart still looked unconvinced as he lay on his back warming himself by the fire, whilst Vita nodded encouragingly at every word Loki uttered. "Perhaps we could bargain with them for safe passage through their mountain home?" she suggested eagerly, addressing only Loki now, in the realisation that he was a sure ally to her plan and her only ally if Everhart's expression was anything to go by.

"Oh yes, good idea Vita," spat Everhart sitting up hastily, "I'm sure they are just longing for this dusty jerkin I've got upon my back, or perhaps one of our other treasures such as this lethally, rock hard cheese is a rarity to be sought in their distant Kingdom

We will probably be able to charge a king's ransom for these wonders!"

Loki padded silently over to his sceptical friend and bumped his huge head against his bearded chin companionably to calm his anger. "Come now Ever, we've got to be positive on a journey such as this," he purred encouragingly, "I think I could barter safe passage from them for a reading you know. I know I've never done one, not seriously and not for anyone other than you or me before but I also know I've the ability to do it and with their fascination for collecting and hoarding knowledge I'm sure they couldn't resist an opportunity to learn more about themselves and their future? We've got to try it if we want to move on haven't we."

The suggestion was a valid one, Everhart was aware of that. But he was also aware that this plan involved putting his greatest friend in danger, not to mention his faithful, if irritating companion Vita and himself. All he had in the way of weaponry was his old sword and knife that he kept at his waist and he didn't think Vita had anything with her more dangerous than an old belt knife worn and rounded at the end and mostly used for cutting bread and cheese. He sighed resignedly and pushed himself up off the ground with his knees. "Best get some sleep then if you two are set on this mad mission. If we wake early enough then I'm pretty sure we can make the mountains by nightfall. I'll take first watch, if no one has any objection." Loki and Vita nodded their agreement as he strode off towards a small hillock to gain a better view of the surrounding area through his watch and to pray earnestly that they would be able to find a safe-haven for Loki soon.

*****

The small curved blade neatly sliced Everhart's jerkin as it whistled past and thunked into the arid, tough earth next to his worn boot. "Stop!" he hissed sternly stretching a protective arm out in front of Loki and Vita who had been chatting merrily as they strode beside him. Vita crouched down readily into a fighting stance, although she hadn't a clue who she was supposed to be fighting or even in what direction she should face. She fumbled to free the belt knife at her waist as she glanced down quickly to eye the wicked blade sticking in the ground at their feet.

Everhart spoke quickly as his eyes darted around wildly. "It was just a warning shot Vita or else I don't think it would have missed me, stand up and look unafraid but don't antagonise them" instructed Everhart in a low voice, standing tall and letting his hands drop to his sides, but not too far from his sword in case things turned ugly.

After a few moments, a pack of three lizard-like creatures that could only have been the Decona from the legends appeared in front of the three travellers. They were incredibly tall and slender creatures with toned muscles that glistened under their silvery green scales as they stepped warily closer. Vita was only mildly surprised to see them walking on two feet; after all, she was the one who had taught their legend to Everhart. They were bare from the waist up but wore a metallic cloth around their waists and the metal chinks of it twinkled in the cool moonlight creating an almost mystical effect when placed next to their captivating scales. Vita could also see tight loops of the metal material wound around their upper legs which secured an alarming amount of small, curved blades - identical to the one that had narrowly missed Everhart a mere moment ago. Instead of simple claws as she had expected, the Decona had fingers and thumbs similar to those of a human, although these were webbed and each was furnished with a long, thin talon with a razor-sharp edge not to dissimilar to Loki's claws. They looked deadly and beautiful - a dangerous combination.

The largest of the Decona trio stepped a pace in-front of its two companions and cocked its head to its right shoulder like a curious cat unsure of what prey it had in front of it. A long, pink, forked tongue shot out of its mouth and back in again tasting the air around Everhart. It lent over to Vita and did the same, and then stopped in front of Loki. "We have memories of you golden one" it nodded in an oddly metallic but musical voice "but not memories of you with dull-eyed, two-legged humans? In what manner are these humans travelling with you? You should avoid them as do we."

Loki took one proud stride forward towards the Decona and spoke clearly and unafraid in a voice that was almost regal "These two are not like other humans that your kind may have come into contact with throughout your history. They are friends of mine and no danger to you Lady Shesha. Unless of course, you pose a danger to them." Loki cocked his head to one side in a mirror image of the Decona, inviting her to decide whether she would be friend or foe.

The Decona blinked two sets of eyelids and cocked its head to one side again; its webbed hand gripped the curved blade it had retrieved from the ground more tightly as it spoke, although its voice sounded more curious than threatening.

"How do you come to know my name Soothsayer? No-one but the Decona know the Decona's names and we have spoken to none other than ourselves for centuries, hiding in plain view of these humans."

"Lady Shesha, your noble name wandered into my head not an hour ago but I do not profess to know you and your kind. However, I can sense the deserved confidence and pride that surround you. I feel you will do well for your people but if you wish I can do a reading for you to tell you more, if, of course, you and your people will guide us safely through your home to save us the perilous journey over the top of your mountain home?"

Shesha's grip lessened slightly on the curved blade as she considered Loki's offer with evident interest. "I will discuss this offer with my people Soothsayer," she sang melodically after a moment, "you will stay here, Do not come forth without my word or you will die. I will come to you with our decision."

The three Decona turned their backs on the trio of travellers and were out of sight within seconds without a hint of noise and without leaving any visible clue as to which direction they had gone in. Vita let out a shaky pent up sigh of relief as she placed a slender hand upon Loki's warm back "Who would have guessed that the lead one was a bloody girl!" she giggled nervously.

Everhart let out a throaty laugh, made louder through his nervousness as he knelt down and pulled Loki and Vita into his embrace "Trust you to think of something as trivial as that!" He guffawed, "I was more concerned as to whether we were going to be speared and roasted but I guess I had assumed she was a he-warrior as well! How the hell do they tell the difference?" He nuzzled his head against Loki's cheek as if he were a great cat himself as he chuckled. "I trust you can do this Loki," he whispered more softly after his relieved chuckling had died down, "and you can trust me to protect you and Vita to the last. I swear it on my life."

"Alright, alright" rumbled Loki's throaty purr as he ducked his head out of Everhart's reach, "no need to go and get all sentimental on me Ever. But if you are that intent on protecting me, you can protect me from my rumbling stomach and dish out some of that awful stale bread and cheese you have festering in the bottom of your haversack before I get down to the serious business of taking a nap before the Decona return. Soothsayer's need their beauty sleep don't you know - I don't look this exquisite without a little effort!"

The party smiled and settled down patiently on the unforgiving ground as they shared some simple fare and awaited the return of the Decona and their fate.

4

A humourless laugh.

"My good Sir, you will take the three silver pieces for the book or nothing at all and I would be remiss if I did not point out that I don't see a whole lot of business trailing through this deserted path. Not even enough footfall for anyone to miss a useless, distasteful cretin like you...well at least not for enough time as it has taken for your bones to be picked clean by those delightful ravens that circle over yonder in the night sky."

*****

Willian whistled with genuine merriment as he twirled his plain, yet clearly effective knife between his thumb and forefinger of his right hand and tucked the heavy, worn book under his left arm with care. It gave him so much more pleasure when he was opposed by these selfish people and could justly rid the world of their inherent greediness and wanton evil. Once he had executed the miserly hermit he had briskly ordered The Unfortunate to haul his body out into the cool night air in order to share it with the night creatures. No-one could call Willian Leroy Liew selfish he thought to himself as he strode under the necessary cover of the eerie forest with The Unfortunate close at his heels, in search of a place to settle down and inspect his newly acquired book. Not like the ghastly merchant who hadn't wanted to share his knowledge for the greater good - or that cursed Everhart! But, he would make him and that abomination that he knew Everhart had selfishly kept to himself since he was a child pay dearly!

The large, flat rock that served as his seat was cold and damp and speckled with soft, swampy green moss, but he was a man who could endure slights such as this on the way to his just and ethereal goal. He delicately turned each yellowed page of the ancient book, being careful to minimise the risk of the old, dried-out pages from breaking up and valuable knowledge being thoughtlessly discarded. Perfect diagrams of the grossly malformed lizard people detailed each part of their hideous bodies with precision and aiding Willian in deciding the weakest spot to strike, should he encounter any of these abominations during his travels. A tiny soft spot at the side of the skull, just underneath where an ear should be on a human was labelled on each side indicating how the creatures heard. Willian's hand absent-mindedly wandered behind his earlobe and smoothed the soft spot between his skull and the curve of his ear. He would keep this in mind if he had the fortune to encounter these almost mythic creatures. Surely this would be the best place to strike to do away with any of them? The next page was more interesting by far for Willian, though, despite his love of efficient butchery. The once brilliant, bright red inks on the page were now faded to a dull burgundy but still detailed the legends of how knowledge was passed on between each generation of the lizard people.

"So whichever Decona consumes of the blood of another shalt know all his knowledge and thoughts as if they had always been his own, thus preserving the learning and reasoning of generations."

Willian was somewhat irritated that the author of this book seemed to credit the creatures with thoughts, feelings and intelligence as if they were human beings equal to himself. Nevertheless, he would force himself to read on if it helped him with his plan. Willian's plan was simple. He would drink the blood of the Decona and find out where that infuriating peasant was concealing the future-seer! He imagined that all these abominations knew where others like them were and would be able to locate them in an instant. Surely what worked for a base species such as the Decona would work successfully for a more advanced being like him and he was sure Everhart and his companions would head towards the mountains next and other creatures that shouldn't be, like themselves. All he had to do was use his trusty blade to pierce that sweet soft spot behind one of the creature's scaly ears and the knowledge of the whereabouts of Everhart and his good fortune would be his for the taking!

Willian glanced up and eyed The Unfortunate who had now sat

upon the dusty ground close to him and was staring off into the distance with a vacant expression on its face. He supposed he had better get it to drink some of The Decona blood as well when the time came. It was stupid enough as it was, and he would need it to be able to keep up with him when the hunt began properly. He may prove useful with delegated tasks despite his lack of ambition.

*****

The perfectly scaled skull of Shesha Decona cocked to one side once again as she waited for the acceptance of her terms from Loki. It irked Everhart that she deferred to him as their leader now instead of himself. It was not that he did not trust Loki, far from it, but he thought of himself as the leader and protector in this trio and was certain he knew best how to keep the three of them safe from harm. Ceding control to someone else left him feeling helpless and on edge. He was mulling over these irritations thoughtfully when Loki's deep voice roused him.

"Done," rumbled Loki's voice throatily, "but my companions will want those weapons returned to them once we pass through your kingdom Lady Shesha, for they may well have need of them once we reach the other side. I am not anticipating an easy journey for any of us."

Shesha's thin scaled lips curved back in a parody of a smile,

"For what use these trinkets are it surprises us that you would want them returned at all friend. I do not know what damage you will do with one worn, old sword and some rounded belt knives," she sang, "if your reading pleases us perhaps we will give you better weapons Soothsayer, although you yourself truly need none other than what you already possess."

Loki dipped his head slightly in acknowledgment and acceptance of the compliment. Shesha seemed pleased by this and waved her webbed hand, motioning the trio to follow her over the arid plains towards the Decona's mountain home. In spite of his ever growing nervousness, Everhart's heart fluttered excitedly at the prospect of seeing inside the home of the legendary Decona race. His parent's had always talked about them with such fever when he was young and imbued in Everhart a deep respect for their place in the world. Everhart had revelled in their fireside stories as his father had described all the legendary creatures that made up the world to his 'little Knight'. Everhart had always aspired to be worthy of his father's nickname for him, trying to always make the honourable choice no matter how much it irked him at times.

The strength of Vita's elbow to his ribs told Everhart that it probably wasn't the first time she had nudged him and he had probably been nodding along with a blank expression for some time to words that he hadn't fully heard, lost in days gone by.

"I said what do you think of it you great dullard!" Vita

questioned Everhart in a low but excited voice, "Don't just nod at me blankly! Can you believe it after all the times we have spoken of it?"

"Think of what!" Everhart retorted irritably as he trudged on. He knew he shouldn't allow himself to be bothered at Vita's constant name calling. That was just the way she was, but he certainly wasn't a dullard and he wished she would just appreciate his efforts at times.

She slowed her pace just enough to perch her hands on her slender hips in typical Vita style as she let out a deliberately slow, exasperated breath as if she was about to explain something to a small child that couldn't seem to understand her words.

"This precious dandelion that I've just crushed with my boot! Oh sorry...wait, I actually meant the towering, glittering Lizard cave with the bloody great welcoming committee standing outside obviously!" Everhart followed Vita's wide-eyed gaze. He had been so lost in his thoughts that he hadn't noticed how far they had walked. The awe-inspiring mountain seemed to glitter with a silvery shimmer up close, much as the scaly skin of the Decona did. It possessed no great door as an entrance, only a huge, gaping gap missing from the rock, which strangely only made the place look more enchanting. A score or more of Decona stood shoulder to shoulder either side of the opening. Not many of the Decona were dressed as Shesha and her companions were. The majority wore thin, silken robes of a golden hue that rippled in the evening breeze. Although Everhart didn't discount that there was the chance that weapons could have been concealed, it did not seem likely underneath the clingy material.

The party of travellers halted in front of the gathering of Decona. Shesha and her two followers stepped away from Everhart and his two friends and joined the rest of their brethren before the mountain entrance. Shesha then addressed the trio as if she had never encountered them before, and it was clear that she spoke as a leader on behalf of her people.

"Welcome to our home ancient friends," she sang loudly, her strong voice carrying well on the air and reverberating off the mountain face. "Please allow us to care for your needs as if they were our own whilst you dwell with us. Rooms have been prepared for guests such as yourselves to refresh themselves after an arduous journey. We would be grateful if you would meet with us in the gathering hall after you have made use of them to discuss with us your reasons for being here and asking of our help."

Shesha and the gathered Decona then bowed deeply as one to the trio. Everhart was rescued from his worry of how to respond to the gesture when Loki stretched his front legs low in imitation of the Decona's bow and replied in his powerful, rumbling voice.

"Whilst I do not know if there are any formal words that I should speak in this exchange, being separated from your kind in my lifetime, let me simply say that we are extremely grateful for your hospitality Brothers and Sisters of the Decona and do swear that we will honour and respect you and your ways whilst we are in your care in your home. We will also be more than willing to discuss a form of payment to offer you in reparation for your aid on our journey."

Shesha's mouth rose in a curve similar to a human smile as she nodded her assent and turned to lead the way inside the towering mountain. The inside of the mountain was comfortably cool and surprisingly well furnished, despite the fact that it had no front door. The walls were covered here and there with thick wall hangings that seemed to depict different Decona scenes from ages gone by. Alcoves had also been chiselled into the rock to allow fat, yellow candles to be placed to light the way along the corridors. As Everhart looked around he quickly began to re-evaluate his first impressions of the Decona people. These were not some hoard of hard-headed, barbaric lizard people but an intelligent and educated race that had somehow managed to keep hidden for centuries mere miles away from human habitation, although from the articles littered around it seemed that their species had not always been so isolated from others.

"We assumed that you would be more comfortable sharing a room instead of being separated from your kin." Shesha sang as she gestured towards a heavy, timber door set into the rock. As

Everhart glanced past her webbed hand he spied at least another dozen doors almost identical to this one, evenly spread out down the corridor. At one time then, had the Decona had frequent guests?

Loki stepped in to cover Everhart's lack of response. "A correct assumption, Lady Shesha, we are more than happy with this arrangement. We will certainly appreciate the comfort of knowing where each other is."

Shesha heaved the door open with one solid push of her muscular arm but did not enter the room herself. Instead, without another word, herself and her attendants swivelled around and marched at a steady pace back the way they had come, leaving the trio to themselves for the time being.

Loki was the first to stride into their allotted room. He called over his shoulder in playful mocking tone as he did so. "And there was me thinking you wanted to be the leader Ever. Couldn't even muster a response to a courteous question. Tut tut!"

5

"How long are we supposed to wait!" grumbled Everhart ungraciously as he rolled onto his hard belly and propped himself up on his elbows with an exasperated sigh.

"Well perhaps you should have inquired about that before, oh noble Leader of ours," smirked Loki teasingly from the middle of the generous, soft, feather-filled bed that he had claimed for himself immediately upon entering the room. Despite his vast size, the tiger had curled up much as a common house cat does. His great, shining black nose was pressed against his thick, orange and black striped tail that had curled itself around his balled body perfectly. Before Everhart could fling a flippant response back at the great cat, Vita hopped nimbly off the bottom bunk of some elaborately carved bunk beds where she had been perched and practically skipped over to a laden, heavy bookcase that had been expertly bolted into the rock walls of their room.

"Don't smart, Ever. Aren't you the least bit in awe of all we have seen here?" She picked up a random volume from the thick bookshelf and opened it up to reveal some richly illustrated pages that seemed to depict some winged creature she had never seen before alongside a man with fire and ice floating around him. "I know that we cannot read the language that these books are written in but just look at the detail my friend. Imagine how much knowledge we could take from them if we were to study them for a long enough time."

A raspy yet still musical voiced bounced in from the now open doorway "That knowledge is not meant for you at this time travellers. Maybe, not ever." A stooped Decona dressed in more humble, cotton robes than the Decona that had awaited them outside the mountain when they had arrived earlier spoke from the entrance. Everhart supposed from his worn voice that he must be elderly but how you were supposed to tell underneath all those scales Heaven only knew. His scales seemed to be just as bright as Shesha's and hadn't dulled with age, if this creature was even old as Everhart knew it at all.

Blinking different sets of eyelids the Decona then began again in a more formal tone. "Lady Shesha requests your presence in the gathering hall at your earliest convenience." It uttered no further words or pleasantries but made no attempt to move back down the corridor or proceed into the room but stood patiently in the doorway.

Everhart assumed 'at your earliest convenience meant right this minute and obviously this escort was non-negotiable. He rolled off the bed with light-heartedness and a ready smile that he did not feel and called to his companions, "Right, everyone ready?"

He set off behind the Decona, knowing full well that he was not ready in the slightest. He had lived in Aither, surrounded by the bright air for all of his live and the biggest villain he had had to deal with was old miserable Barley. He just hoped that he learned how to deal with difficult situations as quickly as possible to make sure he protected his friends instead of dragging them further into danger.

*****

Willian ensured that he didn't approach the mountain too closely at first. He didn't want to arouse any suspicion at this stage and he certainly didn't want to be within eyesight of anything that had its den there and to be perfectly honest with himself, he wasn't even quite sure that this was the place he was supposed to be anyway! The only solid thing that had led him here was a few notes in his newly acquired book that briefly mentioned 'rocky outcrops' in the same section covering the Decona and their usual habitats. The village of Aither and the majority of the surrounding area was mostly wooded and green. This old mountain was the only place that had sprung to mind and being as humans had a tendency to avoid it - for no known reason, suspiciously Willian added to himself - he had supposed it was a good place to start. They must have fled to others more akin to themselves.

He lay belly down on the damp earth behind a small hillock and some unappetising, dry, thorny bushes that possessed no leaves, waiting and watching for an opportunity. He had managed to encourage The Unfortunate to do the same by giving up a filthy scrap of bread, gone slightly mouldy now, that he had dug out of the corner of his haversack with a slim fingernail. The constant night noises that never seemed to bother The Unfortunate, soon settled into a routine and Willian soon ceased to be startled by them despite his distaste for the dark and the night-time creatures it concealed in its shadows. In fact, he was soon so relaxed that his eyelids became heavy and his head began to drop as he nodded off. The bright flash of light dazzling through the tiny gap in his hooded eyes quickly made him jerk his head up as he became fully alert if momentarily confused. What was it and which direction had it come from he wondered breathlessly?! Willian dug his tidy, curved nails deeply into the palms of his hands in an effort to make himself concentrate more and focus on finding the source of the light. His small, black eyes scanned the moonlit horizon frantically as he sought the dancing light. He very nearly missed it but then the object moved again causing the moonlight to shoot back in his direction. A lone lizard-man purposefully moved towards the looming mountain face. Willian noted that it wore some kind of rudimentary metal over its skin that caused the moonlight to reflect off it creating a more mystical effect. Well, these less evolved creatures were often attracted to shiny things weren't they? Much like scavenging crows and magpies Willian thought with disgust -

everyone knew that they were servants of demons and ghouls. Well, on a positive note, now that he knew he was this close to the base beasts he could begin to hatch a plan to kill one and drink its blood. Everything was coming together nicely and neatly just as Willian liked it. A smile curved his mean lips and scarily noticed one appear upon the cracked lips of The Unfortunate in response.

6

Everhart had had to admit that Loki had excelled at their meeting with Shesha and the rest of the Decona in the gathering hall. The companion that he had grown up with in the safety of Aither's forest had finally revealed himself as the true soothsayer that he had been born to be. Loki had begun the meeting himself by sharing with Shesha the visions that had been presented to him regarding himself, Everhart and Vita whilst urging her to realise that this danger posed to himself due to his almost mythical status, applied also to the race of the might Decona who were themselves beginning to be forgotten from human history and enter into the realm of legend. His visions regarding the actual Decona themselves had been vague but after holding the hand of Lady Shesha under his heavy paw, Loki had seen a Decona that was not a Decona, as he put it. He could not explain the vision to her any clearer than that, but warned her to beware of imposters that were not all that they seemed to be. Nevertheless, despite the vagueness of the information, he peppered his reading with enough subservient compliments and awed comparisons to the Decona - always with the comparisons of other races paling in the shadow of the honour and valour of the Decona - to ensure that the warning didn't just leave a sense of foreboding and a bitter taste with the Decona but also with a strong sense of pride and determination to overcome any great malice that was heading their way. In fact the speech had even enthused Everhart himself with an all-encompassing feeling of God-like invincibility. He felt like he was a dutiful knight in the ancient tales that his father used to tell him, with the power and courage to protect his friends against any foe. A heady feeling of heat built up in his arms until he felt he could shoot fire from his fingertips. He supposed he was just getting caught up in the moment along with Loki and the Decona but it felt good to feel optimistic for a change.

Shesha had been so grateful to Loki for a reading that she only knew was possible from ancient memories that she had marched the great tiger along with Everhart and Vita down to the revered Decona armoury herself and beseeched them to pick whichever weapon they desired to keep for themselves. Vita had quickly chosen a curved bow that appeared to be constructed not out of wood, but of the same graceful, glittering metal that fashioned many of the Decona's toga-like clothes. Despite this, the bow was astonishingly light and strapped to Vita's back with no effort at all. Vita had said she could shoulder it for days and not feel fatigued. Shesha presented it to Vita along with an ornate quiver complete with more than a dozen arrows crafted of the same mysterious metallic substance. The quiver, made of a strong smelling, sturdy leather, was stitched with a golden thread depicting many Decona on the backs of great bull-like creatures, their well-formed muscles pulled taught ready to release a volley of arrows. Upon studying the detailed depictions, Vita noticed a minute pocket stitched carefully into the base of the quiver. Shesha calmly informed Vita that this hidden pocket held a deadly poison. The Decona would dip the tips of their arrows into it when in battle to ensure that if a foe did somehow manage to escape them, then they certainly wouldn't get far enough to cause them any further trouble. A most efficient way of eradicating enemy scouts Shesha confided. Vita had gravely thanked Shesha for the gift and vowed to use the poison wisely.

    Everhart erred in his assumption that Loki would find no use in his trip to the armoury for his mind had never seen or imagined the like of the contraption that the tiger chose. It was almost a leather harness that fitted only the tail. Once fitted onto Loki, the tip of his tail became a deadly weapon as a curved silver spike, made of the rare Decona metal, jutted into the air at a killer angle. At least this provided Loki with more protection from behind in a fight mused Everhart, although he always intended to have the tiger's back, and despite Loki's gentle nature he was beginning to think that the cat wouldn't hesitate in bringing his deadly fangs and talons into a fight.

    The blade that Everhart chose seemed as if it had been made with him in mind. It was a huge broadsword that to the eye looked to be extremely weighty and surely taxing to wield. However, when Everhart handled the blade it seemed no heavier than his belt knife, and like Vita, he felt like he could wield his weapon for hours without becoming tired. The hilt was set with four glittering, green emeralds on each side, cut into perfect, symmetrical diamond shapes and bound with the sturdiest brown leather imaginable. The scabbard and belt that accompanied it were equally well embellished, but not with Decona as was the case with many of the weapons in the armoury, but with a proud image of a tiger and human warrior stood side by side. At first, the vast wealth of the sword dissuaded Everhart from taking it from the Decona, yet Shesha had calmly laid a webbed hand on his bulky shoulder and whispered in her singsong voice into his ear

"If you kept the memories of your ancestors as we do Knight, you would realise that this weapon already belongs to you. Take it so that it can be returned to its rightful place. We have kept it hidden from undeserving eyes for as long as has been needed."

Everhart had been too fearful to ask how she knew his father's pet name for him or any more at all, and the mischievous glint in Shesha's brilliant bronze eyes led him to believe she would speak no more on the subject anyway. Perhaps Loki had mentioned it to her when he had been lost in his thoughts on the way here. That seemed like the obviously reason.

"Now step forth companions and continue your life-changing journey," Shesha sang, "we wish you much good fortune on your way. May your weapons and your hearts remain true."

With that, a procession of Decona led Everhart, Loki and Vita slowly through the lengthy, winding corridors of their mountain home, that surely only a Decona could navigate and negotiate and not get lost along the way, and out into the sweet night air on the other side. Everhart took a deep breath, still feeling optimistic that their journey would have a happy ending after all. He turned around, back towards the towering mountain and his hosts to thank Shesha and her Decona for their generosity and aid but they had already gone, faded back into the mountain leaving the trio alone again.

7

After camping out amongst the lifeless, thorny bushes for several days and nights with his freakish companion, Willian was confident of the routine of these lizard-like abominations. They did not seem to venture out of their rocky den in the daylight hours so no wonder humans had started to disbelieve that they had ever existed, but instead small numbers of lizard men - no more than three at a time - seemed to make a cursory patrol of the perimeter in the night, particularly during twilight. This seemed extremely odd to Willian, surely lizards were meant to bask all day idly in the sun? This was just further evidence that these base creatures were un-natural as far as Willian was concerned. Any higher deity would thank him for ridding the world of any of a race that couldn't behave in a proper, orderly manner. As far as Willian was concerned, crepuscular creatures were demon children, un-natural dark worshipers that deserved eradication.

The sudden realisation that dawn was breaking pulled Willian from his musings and gave him the sudden urge to get on with his task as quickly as possible. It was simply because he was sick of being in this barren landscape He wasn't nervous. Not really. Heroes didn't get nervous. That fluttering feeling in his stomach was most likely the result of poor rations after camping out in the damp for so many days with only a twisted, dumb creature for company. He hadn't wanted to chance hunting whilst observing the lizard-men in case they had been alerted by any death cries of potential meals, and he really couldn't trust The Unfortunate to hunt quietly either. Who knew what sort of eerie hearing those devil spawn possessed. The thought of killing brought Willian's knife into a firm grip yet concealed in the palm of his clenched hand as he carefully made his way down from his subtly hidden hillock towards the leering rock face. He whistled lowly for The Unfortunate to follow him, which it did immediately. No grand plans to gain entry had crossed Willian's mind during his time of reconnaissance and so he had decided to simply knock the wall at the entrance at a time when fewest of the lizards were likely to be about. Surely this would appear to the lizards to be the least aggressive option and least likely to provoke a violent or defensive response? He didn't want to walk into an ambush by walking into the lair un-announced and he was sure The Decona with their supernatural abilities should hear him. If all went sour he planned to leave The Unfortunate behind as a distraction whilst he made a run for safety.

His chalk-white knuckles seemed miniscule against the unyielding, cold, thick rock that they rapped upon and the small knocking sound that they produced seemed pathetic, barely mustering an echo. Willian waited for several minutes that seemed like an eternity whilst nervously peering into the bleakness, and had nearly decided to retreat; thinking that maybe Everhart hadn't brought his escapee's this way at all when the echoes of skittering claws could be heard approaching from within the daunting entrance gap. Gulping down a brief moment of fear, Willian was unsure whether to quickly retreat or stand his ground. Before he had arrived at a concrete decision, a small lizard like creature appeared in the dim entrance, the fact that this creature appeared to be only a child of its race returned to Willian his arrogance and over-bearing confidence. He was smarter by far than these primitive beings and no youngling would oppose him.

Willian pointed at himself and then tried to communicate with the animal much to his distaste. "Human!" he gestured at himself wildly. He didn't include The Unfortunate in his gesticulations as he wasn't entirely sure the thing was human anyway and he didn't want these creatures, even a child of one of them, to pick him up in a lie so early on. He then held up two slender fingers, "Two like me. Have you seen them? With a beast?" Willian tried baring his round teeth in a parody of a tiger in an attempt to demonstrate what he was searching for feeling utterly ridiculous for lowering himself to this necessary act. Even The Unfortunate seemed to be looking at him in a more confused manner than normal.

The short lizard cocked its head to one side and blinked steadily twice, making Willian wonder if he was wasting his time entirely and ponder whether to cease this nonsense and instead to leave and search the arid plains again or whether to simply kill the creature anyway in order to see what it was like. He had never had the pleasure of killing a creature like this before and maybe one of its long claws could be retained as a souvenir.

Willian nearly jumped out of his pale skin when the creature spoke in coherent, if eerie sounding words. Never a more blatant sign of black magic had he seen in all his years.

"Surely you cannot be a friend of the great soothsayer and his Knight when you speak so strangely dull-eyes" sang the youthful beast with a hint of contempt in his voice.

The derogatory comment at the end of the abominations utterance restored Willian's aplomb to him as he retorted in a testy voice. "I most certainly am boy! Now I suggest you take me to Everhart Bovenwater and the cat immediately before I lose my patience with you entirely!" Willian held his hands firmly against his hips to exaggerate his annoyance. There was nothing like a sense of drama and hyperbole to instil fear into a youngster. This worked a treat with the dirty peasant brats of Aither, particularly with The Unfortunate looming behind him, and quickly sent them scattering whether to do his bidding or get out of his way as he decided fit.

The Decona raised one corner of its lipless, scaled mouth in an apparent smirk. "You are not welcome here and cannot enter" he whistled and turned on his glittering heel to retreat back into the darkness. Probably to report to an older creature with more authority thought Willian.

Willian's anger, never slow to ignite burst forth and before he even realised what he was doing his knife was gripped tighter and he thrust it with relish into the beast's skull where an ear should have been on a human. Thick dark blood burst forth from the wound, pumping out in a cascade like a crimson waterfall. The creature immediately collapsed to the stone floor with a faint whimper and lay twitching as the hot, dark liquid continued to flood out spoiling the cleanly swept floor. Willian quickly realised that the blood was being wasted. Blood he needed in order to continue in his righteous quest. Damn him - why had he not thought to bring some kind of container with him to keep the liquid in? Kneeling next to the now still and already cooling corpse, Willian cupped his hands together to make a bowl and held them underneath the wound in the lizard's skull, allowing the swirling liquid to pool there, although some of the sticky fluid managed to creep through the cracks in his fingers and trickle down his thin wrists. Surprisingly it smelt pleasant and not like blood at all. It was a rich, warm scent, almost like cinnamon and as Willian stared at it he was sure he saw swirls of sliver glittering in the blood almost like it had been mixed with a molten metal. Still kneeling, Willian raised his cupped palms to his lips and hastily gulped the warmness down. Surprisingly, he noticed The Unfortunate kneel to the ground and do the same without any encouragement. He didn't want to waste any of the blood in an effort to move him away, and he had wanted the creature to taste some of it in order to be able to keep up with him anyway so he stolidly ignored it whilst he scooped up as much blood as he could.

The smell of The Decona blood had made him expect a pleasurable taste, however Willian instantly felt violently sick as the stuff burned him all the way down worse than the cheapest grog he had every sipped. Sing song words echoed through his mind. "Not meant for you…" they whispered. Almost immediately a cramp assailed and caused him to stumble and clutch at the ground and his stomach simultaneously as his vision of the world tilted crazily. He had to get away! If the other lizards discovered him in this weakened state he would stand no chance against those long claws! He clambered ungraciously back the way he had come, not caring if The Unfortunate followed him or not, nearly crawling upon the ground as he sought refuge and wondered whether he would perish in the dirt before he had even properly begun his journey.

8

On this side of the great mountain the land was more fertile, more green and more luscious than anything the companions had ever had the fortune to lay eyes on before. Everhart had no inkling as to why this natural affluence would be so across the Decona's home but he couldn't deny what his own eyes saw.

"It's because this is where the magic begins. The other side of the mountain and Aither have abandoned magic." Loki had said softly as if in reply to Everhart's silent thought. Everhart hadn't asked him to elaborate, the softness of Loki's voice had let Everhart know it was simply one of those seer thoughts that had strayed from his mind to his lips without the cat even realising. Everhart possessed complete faith in his companion and the thought of opposing his views was simply unthinkable to him.

The party slowed their pace down significantly for the first day of their travels on the other side of the mountain, simply to give themselves time to appreciate and enjoy the pure richness of their new surroundings. Once or twice during the hours closest to twilight, Everhart had spied trio's of hunting Decona from a distance, returning to their mountain home with their webbed hands laden with numerous fat rabbits, freshly killed. It was no wonder that the Decona almost never encountered the humans of

Aither these days and were thought to be little more than a far-fetched myth by most, for who would bother stepping out on the other side of this magnificent mountain, except perhaps a cursory watchmen, when this awe-inspiring abundance of life and beauty lay just on the other side? And truth be told, not many humans strayed too far in the dark these days and Aither was not known for a great influx of wandering visitors due to it's quiet, generic and uneventful nature.

"Do you know where we are headed Ever?" queried Vita as they strolled carelessly through the calf high grasses, and touching his well-muscled bicep with a delicate light fingered touch, dragging him out of his wandering thoughts. "As even with my stories that I've gathered over the years, I must admit that I know very little of this side of the mountain, except that the race of the soothsayer's is said to live 'past the scaled drinkers of blood', which I think I can safely assume is this way, past the home of the Decona." Vita's eyes flickered briefly over to Loki who padded quietly along a few paces in front of the humans, checking that her words had not bothered him in any way. He had rarely ventured on to the topic of his race with her during their journey and she hadn't liked to pry despite her eagerness to know if he knew if there were any others like him left. She also did not like to risk raising Everhart's ire by pestering Loki either as she had seen that her friend was keenly defensive of the tiger and if she were to be honest with herself, she could not help but feel a slither of jealousy at the closeness between the two. It wasn't that she did not like Loki, for the great cat had won her over almost instantly with his friendly and mellow ways, it was just that she sometimes wished there was more between her and Everhart and at times it felt as if the tiger took attention that she would have liked for herself. The knowledge that this was a silly feeling to behold just served to make her irrationally irritable at times and ensured her anger which was for herself often found itself fiercely flung at those in close proximity to her.

"I can tell you where we are not headed," Everhart retorted cheerily yet determinedly, "Back. We will keep on moving forward until we find some place that is habitable and that I deem is safe enough for Loki and I to remain without being chased by shadows. I'm not hoping for wondrous miracles Vita. I just want a place that we can call home. Once we find it, I will chivalrously escort you back to civilization, don't you worry about that my dear."

Vita stopped abruptly in her tracks. Her hand flew to her hip and Everhart instantly knew from that pose that he had stoked her anger somehow and that he was now likely about to be berated.

"Escort me! How very dare you Everhart Bovenwater! I am not some hired mercenary or bone-headed bodyguard whose contract expires when we reach our destination. Nor am I some willowy female that needs protection from any man. I made my own decision to accompany you and Loki on this journey and if I decide to return to Aither at any time, then that will be my own decision too!" As she spoke, Vita's nostrils flared angrily and the colour in her cheeks rose to an angry pinch of scarlet on her cheeks as her voice grew louder and louder and shakier with each word.

Without pausing to allow Everhart an opportunity to reply, Vita stalked hurriedly off in front, passing Loki in moments, her stiff shoulders and tense back screaming her fury to the world. Surely the hand shooting up to wipe her face was to swat away a blood-sucking bug though, thought Everhart, as Vita wiping away a tear was out of the question. She got angry, not tearful.

Loki backtracked slightly in order to rub his whiskered cheeks against Everhart's out flung hands.

"I swear it gets harder and harder by the minute to try to talk to that damn woman!" bellowed Everhart in exaggerated exasperation, not caring if Vita heard his clipped bitter words, although she was well ahead by now and didn't look likely to slow her pace any time soon. "It's as if she takes every kindness that I speak to her and shakes it out to find hidden barbs that I never intended to put there! What did I say wrong this time?!"

"Her rashness and quickness to react will be her ultimate downfall," Loki calmly stated in a soft, dream like voice.

Everhart gulped, noticing the trance like state his friend issued the words in, but doing his best to ignore it. "Loki, it's not like you to be so judgmental," Everhart mumbled, "even if your words do ring true," squatting down to a more equal level with his feline friend and looking into his deep, emerald eyes.

"I..." Loki cocked his head to one side as if trying to reach for a thought as he struggled for words for a moment. "I didn't even think it Ever. It just came straight out of my mouth from nowhere. Maybe I'm just tired and so speaking without thinking. My eyes itch abominably you know. You couldn't pour some water into them from your water skin to wash them out could you please old friend. I would do it myself, but lack of those clever little thumbs that you possess can make it quite tricky?"

His eyes did look slightly peculiar, Everhart had to agree. It was as if they seemed to be a bit brighter, the greenness of them almost flickering with burning emerald flames. Everhart had never seen them that luminescent before. Come to think of it though, Everhart's eyes had been besieged with a burning sensation ever since they had left the Decona's underground home. Perhaps it was just the impact that was to be expected after spending such a long duration underground when you weren't used to it and then returning to brighter environments. Everhart and Loki had spent most of their lives either in the airy, little village of Aither or gambolling around the beautiful, bright forest that surrounded it and had never even set foot underground. Everhart unstopped his water skin and carefully trickled a little of its contents into the corner of each of Loki's shining, sea-green eyes to give him a little relief.

"Is that any better old friend?" he queried with genuine concern.

"Not really," sighed Loki resignedly, giving a lazy yawn for emphasis, and then shaking his head quickly to dry his eyes.

A high pitched female scream from up ahead reverberated in the open air. Loki's earlier words regarding Vita after she had stalked off echoed through Everhart's mind as he raced after the big cat who had already sped off to reach their friend and face whatever danger had found her.

Braced for the worst, Everhart was slightly puzzled but nonetheless relieved to see Vita sat upon the ground with Loki standing protectively over her when he caught up. He was the fastest runner in Aither by far but even he couldn't outrun a tiger at full speed.

"What happened, Vita? Are you alright?" demanded Everhart breathlessly, his worry from hearing the scream mutating into irritation that he had been caused to fret so much when clearly, Vita seemed unhurt.

Loki dipped his head in the direction in front of them, "See for yourself. The girl nearly went plummeting over the side. Surprisingly though we have nothing worse than a bruised backside to show for it."

Everhart followed Loki's emerald gaze up ahead. The grassy ground did not extend much further, but instead sheared off into a dizzying drop ending in a rushing river below. From the look of it, a sturdy rope bridge had once connected this side of the river to the other. Oddly, the bridge appeared to have been deliberately hacked away from the other side of the river, yet from the amount of plant life that had crept and tangled up to establish itself around the shorn rope, Everhart surmised that this destruction had been carried out a long time ago. It was at least a small comfort that it wasn't an obstacle intended for them specifically. They could do without any surprises.

"You had made me so furious Ever, that I wasn't really watching where I was going," Vita's usually cocky and confident voice sounded a bit shaky and shell shocked to Everhart's ears, although the anger was still in her voice "and I walked straight over the edge. I somehow managed to grasp some of those climbing vines as I did so. I'm just lucky that Loki hauled me up and dropped me on my backside when he did as I don't think they would have held my weight for much longer!"

Despite his empathy for Vita, Everhart did not fail to notice how she had somehow managed to make her walking herself off a cliff his fault instead of her own responsibility! He was about to respond with a nasty comment back but Loki calmly stepped in, as he seemed to be doing a lot of, of late, to steer the boiling situation into another, less antagonised direction.

"Well I suggest that we give Vita a bit of time to compose herself after that little incident and then determine a different path for us to take, as clearly we cannot proceed in this direction." He stated, not looking directly at Everhart or Vita. Vita for once was blissfully quite, so Everhart agreed with a stiff grunt and flopped down to the soft earth, his back towards Vita.

9

The excruciating cramps had lasted several days and nights and had felt like the announcement of death. Willian could do nothing more productive for the duration of them than lay in a clump of leafless bushes and yearn for his life to end quickly. He still felt nauseous and slightly disoriented due to the double vision that appeared to have afflicted him since he drank the creature's still warm blood, almost as if one picture had been laid slightly askew over another identical picture. Yet, he was once more determined to see his noble quest through to its conclusion. Especially now that he possessed even more precious knowledge to aid him on his journey. In the throes of his fever, Willian had been besieged by what he had now come to think of as 'Blood Dreams'. Dis-jointed Decona hopes, thoughts and ideas had assailed him without mercy. Some of what he had been shown was completely useless to him and his quest, such as the flashes of juvenile Decona, similar to the one that he had exterminated, playing some kind of wrestling games together and loudly laughing in an odd, metallic way that reminded Willian of wind chimes bouncing off one another in a cool Summer breeze. Nevertheless, a vast majority of the blood dreams that he had seen had showed Willian inside the lair of the lizard people, along with paths and ways through the mountain disused to the fully grown

Decona, that only the lizard children seemed to be aware of and seldom used for fear of being reprimanded by their elders if they were caught. These secret ways in and out of the mountain that the children used infrequently when playing, intrigued Willian the most out of his visions. This was a piece of knowledge that he could use to his advantage. Obviously the traitor and his mythical cat had been with the Decona on their way to wherever they were headed and therefore, he needed to get through the mountain also if he was to catch up to them and usurp Everhart's obvious plans to use the cat's powers all for himself.

When Willian had fully awoken however, he had discovered lying next to him the cold, dead body of The Unfortunate. One of its twisted arms had been flung over its hideous face, but wasn't enough to hide the dried blood that covered its chin, throat and front of its decimated clothes. Obviously, The Decona blood had been too much for it, thought Willian. The creature clearly wasn't as strong as himself, in body or in mind. Willian had buried the body in a shallow, pebble grave. Not out of compassion, but just so it wasn't easily discovered, in order to give him more time to get through the warren of Decona paths that he had been shown before even more suspicion was aroused.

One such secret path shown in the blood dreams was where Willian found himself at the present time. He had been unable to re-approach the mountain from the main entrance that he had stood outside of days ago, as the entrance gap now bristled with scaly lizard-men that he had seldom caught sight of before, now armed to the teeth with menacing, glittering weapons, whose many sharp blades parried the sun's rays, bouncing them back into his face. Willian personally doubted that this reaction was over any love for the young Decona that he had killed. That was a human response. Surely primitive creatures such as these were incapable of experiencing love. More than likely this display was anger over knowing that a stranger had trespassed within their home. Some beasts were extremely territorial after all. It was best not to go back that way at the moment. Anyway, thought Willian, once he had the power of the seer he could return and eradicate these lizard-like creatures whenever he felt like it.

Willian sighed heavily and rubbed the skin between his forefinger and his thumb roughly. The skin between his fingers had been itching constantly since he had awoken from his stupor and it seemed tender, puffy and swollen and painful to the touch. No doubt he had lain in some poisonous plant whilst he had been recovering from the overwhelming effects of the lizard's blood. Willian hoped to find some cool, refreshing water once he managed to get himself out of this musty mountain to soak his sore hands in. Until then, he thought to himself, he better get himself moving. It was difficult to accurately estimate the time of day or night in this shadow-worshipping place, but Willian was aware that a number of hours must have passed since he had lain down on his stomach in this low-ceilinged corridor after hearing what sounded like footsteps in the distance. His caution had won over and he had decided to let the distance between himself and the soothsayer and his protector Everhart lengthen rather than risk capture by these heathens.

He heaved himself up into an uncomfortable stooping position that was the most room that this disused corridor allowed and slowly proceeded forward with his left arm trailing the cold, damp stone wall in order to help him make his way, and his right hand tightly clutching his knife in case he encountered any Decona trouble. His spine and shoulders ached abominably, almost as if the structure of his entire body was trying to change itself into something else entirely. He decided that the cause of the pain was no doubt due to this ridiculous stance he was forced to adopt in order to make his way through the Decona tunnels. The sooner he was out of this damned place the better.

After what seemed like days of making his way forward in the dim light, struggling to see anything at all, Willian finally saw a shaft of sunshine beckoning to him from up ahead. He quickened his awkward, shuffling pace despite himself and soon emerged into a rocky outcrop that descended into some lush, grassy fields below. As he made his way down, he noticed a slither of silver shimmer running up his left arm. It looked like some sort of metallic residue had embedded itself in his skin. He tried to wipe it away in annoyance to no avail and eventually after a few unsuccessful attempts he dismissed it, surmising that he must have grazed his arm in the dark winding corridors and it was now dirtied with the fine, silvery dust that had seemed to cling to everything in the corridors he had made use of to make his way unseen through the Decona's mountain kingdom. The creatures were obviously content to dwell in their own filth unlike civilized humans.

Once he reached the bottom, Willian glanced about for some water to clean himself up and to have a much needed drink to quench his burning throat. He was disappointed that none seemed to be immediately available, yet on the other hand he brightened at the thought that a water supply could not be too far away if the arable land that was in abundance here was anything to go by. He set out with a lighter heart, and also a lighter back due to the fact that he had seemed to have misplaced all his belongings in his trance induced few days of agony. But there was no need to worry, he thought smiling to himself. He would just appropriate Everhart's belongings after he killed him. The thought almost brought a skip to his step as he carried on through the lush grassland.

10

The unusual trio had surmised that if they followed the fast flowing river as closely as possible, then they would eventually arrive at some sort of manageable crossing point. The immediate problem was in trying to determine which direction to follow the river in. Vita had irritated Everhart by pressuring Loki, insisting that as he was a seer then it followed that he must know in which direction they must go. Everhart had never demanded knowledge from his friend in all the years that they had been together for he knew Loki's generous and kindly nature meant that he would always share what needed sharing. If Loki had known for sure which direction to take, he would never withhold that information. Nagging him just ensured he would feel responsible for anything that went wrong as a result of his decision, thought Everhart irritably. Everhart knew he should protect Loki from these types of pressures. He knew that was what he was meant for, a guardian to Loki.

As the thought formed in Everhart's mind he rubbed a sweaty thumb roughly into his closed eyelid as his eyeballs seemed to burn more uncomfortably in their sockets, the warming sensation nearly unbearable. "I'll be glad when we get to the same level as this damn river," he mumbled, "then I can rinse my eyes out and refill our water skins. I'm unbearably warm, I feel almost as if I am about to burst into flames."

The words were just an idle comment and not a directed question, but Vita still answered them.

"Well if we don't reach the river and a crossing point Everhart Bovenwater, you'll only have yourself to blame. You were the one who chose this way for us after all."

Everhart rolled his eyes at Loki, who suppressed a cat's grin in response to hide his mirth. The two friends walked companionably a few paces in front of Vita, Everhart resting his hand comfortably on Loki's wide back. Everhart had only picked a direction to travel in in order to save Loki from having to do so under the pressure of Vita's misunderstanding. Loki was aware of that fact and was grateful to his friend for the kind action, but Vita just wanted to view the situation as if Everhart was raking control for himself and taking the decision away from her. "Even though she wasn't exactly forthcoming with suggestions." Everhart had earlier observed to Loki in a low whisper, careful not to let the irritable Vita hear his words. Everhart had wondered, not for the first time on this journey, whether it would have been a better idea and definitely more enjoyable if Loki and himself had set out on their own. Not that Vita hadn't been helpful, her skilfully crafted bow had proven to be more than useful in providing rabbits for her and Everhart to eat, and whilst she was off hunting prey for dinner, it gave Everhart the opportunity to find roots and tubers to roast for

Loki to eat without having to go hungry himself. The problem was more that he didn't feel that Loki and himself could be as relaxed and as open with each other as they usually were and Vita had the never-failing knack to stir his irritation up nigh on every time she spoke, escalating everything into an argument.

The trio finally crested a small hill that inclined down into a shallow valley. It certainly looked more promising and Everhart became confident that they would reach the river soon.

"This place seems vaguely familiar," commented Loki slowly, "as if I should know it. I feel, almost, as if I have been here before. Perhaps in another time."

Vita's mouth opened slightly as she drew a breath to reply, but Everhart silenced her with a wave of his hand and a narrowing of his ever-brightening eyes. For a wonder she actually paid heed to Everhart's warning and abruptly closed her mouth, although, the quick folding of her arms in front of her chest betrayed her irritation effectively. Everhart found that he really didn't care. He knew Loki better than she ever could, and once he started talking like this, it was best to let his musings take their course without interruption. When the two companions were younger, Everhart's interruptions often made Loki lose his trail of thought before he reached his conclusion and he had complained that they muddled his visions, making it difficult for him to recollect them in the correct order. Everhart had decided long ago that it was better to remain quiet, just listening, until it was clear whether Loki was just making idle conversation or truly struggling to decipher a seer's vision.

The great cat easily bounced from boulder to boulder as he pounced gracefully down the descending hill with new found energy. Vita and Everhart followed at a respectful distance as Loki's excited mutterings continued. Vita had never seen the seer this animated and she found she was also swept up in his positive energy.

"It seems as if we are getting closer to where we belong Everhart my brother. This is the way home!" The cat trumpeted joyfully.

Loki spoke the words with utter confidence and waited patiently for Everhart to catch him up. When he did, the pair grinned at each other like two overgrown children as Loki's infectious exuberance wrapped Everhart up. The pair almost skipped on, their pace picking up speed as they hurried on to find a place where they both belonged.

"What about me?" asked Vita dolefully. Yet as she looked up for a reply to her question, she realised that the green-eyed pair were already out of earshot. Her brief flicker of positivity and belonging disappeared from her as fast as her two travelling companions were moving out of sight.

11

Willian was not a skilled healer or a physician but he knew something was definitely wrong with him and his body. Whilst he wasn't and was never likely to be as muscly and as strong as the likes of Everhart, he liked to think he was pretty agile and fit and had the durability to keep going for a respectable distance before requiring a rest. He was a proud man and not like some of the lazy inhabitants of Aither that were content to get fatter and fatter with each passing day doing nothing at all to change the course of history for the human race. Yet for the last day or so he had found that he had to keep pausing to catch his breath or to ease a persistent cramp or stitch and each time that he had to stop, the time that he took to recover seemed to lengthen until he almost felt that he was resting more than he was on the move.

At first it had just been the infernal itching across his skin and the increasing puffiness of his hands that had assailed him, but before long, Willian's breathing had become more and more laboured and his muscles felt stretched and tortured as if someone had had him on the rack for days at a time. He could constantly taste the metallic tang of blood in his mouth and his spit was tinged with an angry pink colour. Willian had never really got sick before, not even as a child had he been ill when all the other children were suffering with the standard illnesses one suffered in youth, but he found since he had awoken from his painful slumber that he had been unable to stop himself vomiting down his jerkin on more than one occasion. His feet and ankles were so badly swollen that after removing his worn boots to inspect the cause of the swelling, he had been unable to fit his boots back onto his painful feet and had instead had to abandon his footwear and walk barefoot through the grasses. Something was definitely not right inside of him.

Willian had been sat in his current position for a good hour or more, but he had felt much too weary and abused to rouse himself. He lifted his throbbing head from his itching arms and held them straight out in front of himself, despite the pain this induced to take a good look at them and see whether his 'condition' had progressed any further. His skin now seemed to have taken on a greyish, silvery cast and it felt tight and dry to the touch. He was sure if he could bathe and he scrubbed his arms, a great quantity of his skin would come away with the soap. An image of a snake shedding its skin entered Willian's mind and he was both angry and relieved that he did not have a shaving mirror in his possession at the present moment in time, for whilst he had an irresistible urge to look at his painful face, he feared that he knew what would be staring back at him. Especially if the accelerated change in the rest of his body was anything to go by.

Wearily and with great effort, he pushed himself up with his creaking knees that screamed angrily in protest, as he forced himself to continue his honourable journey. When he caught up with the cowardly runaways, he would learn all their magic secrets and he would make that mangy cat put this horrific abnormality right! Why, it was all his and the thick-skulled bodyguard Everhart's fault anyway! He would make them pay for their heinous crimes against him! They would beg for forgiveness at his feet as he looked down upon them and delivered judgement.

 Willian gasped unexpectedly in white hot pain. He had stoked his own anger so much, that he had balled his right hand into a tight fist and smacked it against the palm of his left hand furiously. He looked down to find the source of his insistent agony and saw bright, crimson blood trickling out between his middle and forefingers. He lifted his wounded hand closer to his face for further inspection and took in a short, shocked, painful breath, for the blood seemed to be oozing not from his actual fingers, but from some neat webbing that appeared to have grown perfectly between each one. It was just like the Decona's...

12

The pleasant walking pace that the trio of friends had adopted recently on their journey had mercilessly evaporated as soon as the heavens had opened with unapologetic abandon and the persistent rainfall had hammered down upon them without mercy. The heavy rain, backed by the daunting dark clouds that loomed over them menacingly in the sky, showed no signs of easing off and Loki absolutely detested getting himself wet, odd as that was for a tiger, although not for the rest of his feline species. His slick, sodden fur now stuck up upon his neck, shoulders and back in rows of perfectly formed spikes in every possible direction, as if to scream out it's irritation with the consistent, thudding rainfall. His expression was in just as miserable a state as his coat of fur and Everhart could easily see that there would be no opportunity to travel further without incident on this night. He resolved to find some shelter from the weather for himself and his companions with due haste. They had no exact timescale anyway being as their destination was not determined at the moment, but still Everhart could not seem to shake the feeling that he needed to hurry.

Vita's high-pitched shout caught his attention, even above the noise of the steady drumming rain.

"Over there!" She pointed, hastily wiping her dripping, brunette tangled hair away from her squinting eyes, as her finger jabbed emphatically ahead of the party into the distant darkness. Her other hand came away with knotty hair, pulled from her chilled scalp and tangled around her fingers where it seemed determined not to become dislodged.

"It looks like some sort of a cave or cavern. Looks like it goes quite deep too so we should be able to get out of the rain even with a driving wind. We can shelter there for the rest of the night and hopefully this damned weather would have eased off by morning and we can get on without getting soaked to the bloody bone!"

"Alright," agreed Everhart easily with much relief in his bass voice, needing no encouragement to find some shelter and feeling content that the solution to the problem that he had just been trying to solve had presented itself so readily, "let's get over there then gang. I could do with getting my feet out of these sodden boots."

"What!" cried Vita incredulously, as her dripping hands, still decorated with tangled wisps of hair, shot to her sodden hips in her irritable manner, as always. "You're just going to wander over to some dark and dank, strange cave without even checking it out first!? Any danger could be lurking in there for us you idiot!" Vita bit her bottom lip in irritation. She knew she sounded irrational but she had hoped for some thanks or some recognition of her worth from Everhart for spotting the cave and not just his ready agreement to shelter there. She wanted him to make a big deal out of making sure she was safe as well, but as this went against her usual independent demeanour, her behaviour always seemed purposefully full of ire.

Loki stoically ignored the sudden argument as he had done with the countless others that he had heard between Vita and Everhart over the course of their journey that had all equally sprung from nothing, and began quickening his pace to a steady trot towards the beckoning shelter of the cave to flee the tiresome rain and disagreements, leaving the other two to get the inevitable bicker that would now happen, over and done with. Loki had to admit that the incessant arguing was beginning to grate on his usually sunny temperament more and more, despite the fact that he was aware that the reason for it was simply that Vita was struggling over how to present her feelings for Everhart to him, and he wouldn't deign to listen to it longer than he had to. Humans, he had decided, had a knack of making everything a lot more difficult for themselves than it had to be. Life could be so simple if they didn't insist on skirting around issues, thoughts and feelings throughout their lives.

"What is your damn problem now Vita! You pointed out the cave yourself you bloody maniac!" yelled back Everhart in complete and utter exasperation, waving his soggy arms theatrically in the air to emphasise his anger. "What is it with you Vita! Do you actually want me to argue with you all the time?! I don't understand you at all, I'm only agreeing with you, you crazed cantankerous woman!" Everhart's outraged outburst was a result of genuine confusion, Vita realised, like most men, he needed anything regarding a relationship spelt out to him plainly. As her mother had often lamented about her father when she was young, if it didn't have teeth to bite him, he would never realise something was there even if it was right under his nose. Nevertheless, the oblivious nature of the man mixed with her embarrassment at her own emotions never failed to exacerbate her edginess and snappy tendencies.

"You are my problem Everhart Bovenwater, you great bonehead! You want to be the one in charge, huh? The almighty leader?! Then you have to be the one to step forth, protect us and show us that you actually care whether we are safe or not! You can't just wander us into dangerous and potentially fatal situations, even if we are eager to dive in. And...and...you can't just abandon people when they cease to be useful to you any longer, when they have left everything that they know behind all for you."

Everhart's mouth hung open and he was slack jawed as he struggled for a clever and witty response that unfortunately managed to elude him. He was utterly dumbfounded by Vita's heartless accusations. He would never, ever, contemplate abandoning anyone, most notably his closest friends. That just wasn't the way he was constructed. The Knight closed and opened his mouth again, resembling a struggling fish on an abandoned beach left behind by retreating water, in an attempt to muster a defensive response when a deafening tiger's surprised roar rumbled out into the damp night air. Only... it wasn't HIS tiger's roar.

Everhart promptly unsheathed his glistening broadsword from its impressive scabbard without hesitation as he ran with powerful, lengthy strides towards the dark cave's entrance and was reassured to hear an arrow being notched to a bowstring as Vita easily kept up pace behind him, their argument forgotten in an instant as they raced to their friend's aid without contemplation of what the danger may be to them.

The two humans skidded into the saturated cave entrance, the dark shadows doing nothing to diminish the perceptiveness of Everhart's glowing green eyes. And what a sight his beautiful eyes beheld! His tiger, Loki, had his broad back to him, standing stock still. His feline friend faced what could only be described as an ancient version of himself.

The opposing tiger was near enough the same size as Loki currently was, if a bit less well-muscled through age, yet he possessed an identical pair of startling bright, green emerald eyes that seemed, unlike the rest of the beast, untouched and undamaged by time and age. The same could not be said for the creature's striped coat of fur. His coat was almost a completely silver-grey hue and was shot through with a few flecks of orange and black here and there as if it was recalling the colour that it once had kept.

His stripes were a slightly darker grey than the colour of the rest of his lank fur, which appeared to be a lot thinner, less glossy and more brittle than Loki's coat, was. Everhart had had no idea that a tiger could live to become such an age that his coat could turn completely grey. Everhart found himself thinking that this must have been an impressive creature in its youth.

The ancient tiger lifted it's brilliant, blazing eyes to gaze at Loki studiously and suddenly his face lit up with the same, 'almost smile' that Loki often pulled for the sole benefit of Everhart.

"So I was right all along!" crowed the old cat victoriously, almost capering around like an excited cub with a true lack of malice to his persona. "A young soothsayer and his knight, still here, still alive, in the folds of history and time."

"Then you are a soothsayer too?" queried Loki anxiously, almost whining. His joyful nature seemed to have become truly subservient and Everhart almost fancied that his great cat would be squirming in front of the grey apparition, baring his vulnerable belly any second now. He, however, had not relinquished his cautiousness or ire and he attempted to take charge of this unfolding situation.

"Why does everyone keep calling me a damn knight!?" he demanded, furiously ignoring Loki's question to the stranger and still irked by his argument with Vita and the sudden panic that had immediately followed induced by a foreign growling, causing him to genuinely fear for his friend's life. His strong fingers curved intimidatingly around the hilt of his blade as he took a determined step forward.

"What I would relish to learn is the reason why everyone keeps bloody ignoring me!" spat Vita venomously "Can you not see this damn great bow that I'm aiming at you grey one!" Despite her worry at the peculiar situation, Vita did not shake at all. The bow was still aimed with perfect steadiness.

Irritating Vita still further, the ancient tiger gave a low throaty chuckle at the situation, apparently discounting its severity, and chortled out "From your puzzled face and words I can see that I have quite a bit of explaining to do. Why don't you lower that bow my friend and I will graciously answer as many questions as I can for you and these two miracles that you are with, that have graced me with their presence and brought newfound joy to my life, something I had never thought to experience again."

Vita instinctively looked to Everhart first and then to Loki, for some direction as to what she should do. She was reluctant to lower her bow, yet this creature seemed to offer no immediate peril towards them. Her two friends nodded in coherent unison, indicating that they felt that they were safe enough for now. Vita slowly lowered her trusty bow, yet remained stiffly standing by the cave's entrance, keeping her cloak of distrust wrapped tightly around her as if it were her only armour.

Loki seemed more in awe of their new acquaintance than anything else as he stared with wondrous eyes at the silver-grey tiger in their presence, and seemed to have abandoned all sense of caution and watchfulness, seeking only answers and acceptance.

"May I ask, how is it that you came to be here, in this bland place Sir?" asked Loki in a serious yet respectful tone, "I thought that I was the only one in the world like myself, for I have neither met nor heard of anyone else like us in all my years."

The silver-grey tiger sympathetically smiled a worn, yellow, toothy, yet melancholy smile. Before he answered Loki, he shifted to make himself more comfortable as he lay down on the cold stone floor of the gloomy cave, curling his tail around his back legs and the pink, shiny pads on his feet.

"I beg you to sit down with me my new friends. This tale is a long and bitter one to tell, so I suggest that you make yourselves as comfortable as you can before I begin it, for I have no patience for interruptions and rudeness." With this, to Vita's astonishment, the wizened old creature actually winked one green eye at her!

Only Loki and Everhart took the ancient creature up on his offer. Vita still insistently retained her perturbed expression. She could see what was happening here, she thought to herself with a heavy heart. Everhart and Loki were becoming more embroiled in a world that she didn't seem to be invited along to. They had found someone else's company that they preferred more than hers and she felt like she was becoming more and more pushed out of the group, sitting alone on the edge of belonging. She mumbled something about going hunting for provisions before she stalked stiffly back out into the harsh, dark, night rain before her emotions could betray her weakness. Everhart offered an awkward apology on her behalf, annoyed at her uncalled for rudeness and kindled a quick fire in the centre of the cave with some stones, dried grass and broken twigs that were littered about the floor of the cave in order to stave off the night's chill fingers.

"Loki Seer and Everhart Knight. Allow me to formally introduce myself and properly make your acquaintance. I am called Mopsus, and as I am sure you have deciphered, I am also a seer and I am truly pleased and honoured to finally meet you both in the flesh, instead of simply in the recesses of my senior mind. Whilst most of our kind experience different visions and rarely see the same vision on more than one occasion, you two have been twisted into my thoughts and entangled into my mind ever since my days as a sprightly, colourful cub. Now that you have finally proved to be as real as I am, I am more positive that there is hope for our kind's survival yet!"

"You think that we can save the species of soothsayers - tigers - like yourself Mopsus?" asked Everhart doubtfully, yet in a friendly tone as if he had been acquainted with this seer for many a year. His tone, however, betrayed his dubious outlook and the fact that he couldn't help but envision that the elderly Mopsus may be slightly addled. "Are there many left besides you, and my friend Loki here?"

Mopsus grinned enthusiastically, "Not just tigers Everhart my friend. I said 'our kind' did I not? I am certain that if seers are returned to us then Knights such as yourselves must be returned to aid this world also. The two are one and there may be some left in our time if we are lucky."

At Everhart's bewildered expression, Mopsus realised that perhaps his new audience weren't quite as up to speed with the truth of what they were as he would have liked or expected considering the incredible nature of what they were.

"Do you truly not know of what you are Everhart Bovenwater? Even with Loki, a seer, here as your companion in this world? Did your peers and family not rejoice over the fact that you were the child born to be the knight of a new seer when you were birthed with telling emerald eyes?"

Everhart shook his head dumbfounded, although still not quite convinced that Mopsus was altogether right in the head. "My father did always used to call me his little knight when I was a young boy, before he and my mother left Aither on a quest, but I thought that it was just an indulgent nickname for a father's only son and child. There are no knights or seers in my tiny, dusty village of Aither, Mopsus, and there never have been - well - for as long as I have lived there anyway - and that is a goodly twenty-six years. My parents left when I was still very young. They told me that they knew in their hearts that I was meant for something more than Aither could provide and they swore that they would return with triumphant news of my destiny. I always thought that they were just over-proud parents, desperate for their son to be important. But they...never came back...I know nothing of 'what I am' as you put it."

"Surely you are not suggesting that you cannot even use your powers as a Knight then?! I find it extremely difficult to comprehend that no-one has ever taught you this, my son?!" demanded Mopsus anxiously in his creaky, older voice. The tip of his tail twitched erratically as he interrogated the pair and his ears pointed towards them in earnest.

"Powers...I...well who would have taught me anything in Aither? Old Barley?!" laughed Everhart bitterly with a wry smile upon his destitute face. "The only one that I ever learned anything from is my friend Loki here. After we found each other in the forest when we were both young, we have been the only ones looking out for each other. We have never had anyone else and never needed anyone else to show us anything thank-you very much! If you mean power as in strength, then I have power enough to have protected Loki this long and sense enough to get him further away from other people when I did."

"Found each other?" interrupted Mopsus incredulously, "You mean to tell me that you weren't even born together? Not even in the same vicinity?"

Everhart and Loki shook their heads in unison. "You do realise that we aren't of the same species don't you Sir? How could a tiger and a human possibly be born together?" The Knight shot his feline companion an uneasy, concerned look as his eyes darted back to the old creature who was questioning them so intently.

"Now that is unknown as far as I am aware," mused the old tiger thoughtfully, thankfully missing the disrespectful glace, "all my visions of you two were together, in a shady forest, right the way from young cubs to as you are here today. Not that anyone else ever believed them mind you, as old as I am, I think they were prone to thinking I was addled in the brain."

The old tiger paused, grinning a knowing smile at Everhart before he continued with a wicked wink.

"Anyway, I had always automatically assumed that you had been born together, as is proper for our kind. I now see from your blank expressions that you are indeed in need of education from the very beginning. You see, it is the way with our kind that each time a new soothsayer is born unto this world; a human is also born in order to protect the new seer's life, as his or her Knight. They are bonded inextricably from birth. Generally, they are born of the union of two ordinary human parents that reside near to a soothsayer settlement. I would hazard a guess that living in such proximity to each other for a lengthy period of time means that some of the seer magic seeps into the soul of the nearby humans. Magic does not take kindly to being confined. When news of a soothsayer pregnancy was announced, which was a rare occurrence you understand, as soothsayers live a particularly long time and in order to balance this, new soothsayer's are seldom born, human women who had fallen pregnant around the same time would arrive to stay with the soothsayer's until the cub and children were born, in the sincere hope that their child would be the one that was chosen to open emerald eyes at their birth. Then they would gift their child to other Knights from the first moment of their very birth in order for them to be educated by other elemental masters and grow up with their own soothsayer. We would care for the human parents from then on as well of course and allow them to remain with us to see the greatness of their child come to fruition. Many of them are useful for their foraging skills not to mention the benefit of their companionship and eclectic way of viewing the world."

Loki was clearly hanging on every word that was uttered by Mopsus with complete admiration in his youthful eyes. Those bright eyes were wide as he whispered "Elemental masters? What does that mean good Sir?"

"It means my dear Loki that your Knight here should have

already been taught and should have long ago been able to manipulate and control the elements in order to protect you and your vitally important visions. I am surprised indeed that without our traditional Knights to educate your Everhart, that he has managed to keep his power contained for this long and not been utterly destroyed by them. There have been a few cases of wayward Knights thinking that they have control of their powers and dealing themselves a fatal injury in my time. The magic has the potential to vanquish all. Did the pair of you not even feel a burning through your bodies from the days of your youth as the powers tried to seek release from their unnatural containment?"

The two friends exchanged secretive glances hesitantly and Everhart absent-mindedly rubbed his tired eyes with a meaty thumb and forefinger.

"Well, just recently" answered Loki slowly, "our eyes have been burning slightly. Although we assumed that it was merely down to spending so much time underground with the lizard-men, the Decona, and then trying to adjust our vision and get our eyes re-used to the natural light when we emerged into the open air and sunlight again."

Mopsus chuckled throatily as his black lips curved into a hearty smile "Well, well, well. If that is the extent of all that you two cubs have experienced unaided and by this age as well, I may well have been more correct than I knew at the time. You pair have the real potential to become the most powerful soothsayer coupling that the world has ever known. You can save us all."

13

The unbearable pain was still there, searing white hot pain, deep inside of him, often making him forget much of his life altogether. Nevertheless, the one thing that he had not forgotten was who was responsible for this malevolent mutation and Willian's hatred burned even more brightly than his pain. He would have his revenge.

Now he had taken to travelling around in the twilight hours instead of under the unforgiving heat of the ferocious sun, just like the crepuscular critters that he despised so much. However, this venomous hatred stopped Willian from making use of his heightened sense to its full benefit. If he breathed out and embraced his new self, everything was so much clearer. In fact, if he relaxed, he was sure he was close to the wretched group that he had set out after so many weeks ago on his quest to appropriate the soothsayer and liberate the human race. Since his transformation had begun, Willian had noticed that some of his senses were incredibly sensitive. His eyesight was much keener, especially in the darkness and the twilight shadows and his sense of smell appeared to have increased dramatically. So much in fact, that Willian was almost positive that he could breathe the smell of human in through his scaled nostrils and taste it on his now lizard-like tongue.

His skin had not managed to escape the rapidly hastening changes either. It was now so hardened and scaly that it had not hurt or blistered in the slightest when he had a spent a day under the shade of an immense tree, among shingles and bracken, fashioning a make-shift blade out of some flinty rock that he had found along his travels. He had no idea exactly how he was going to use this this shoddy weapon, but he damn well knew who he was going to use it on, and he was getting ever closer to that person with every passing minute. He could smell his individual scent on the cool breeze and he knew with a profound certainty that that person had passed this way not too long ago. If he concentrated on his senses he could track him with ease.

The heavy rain was just beginning to ease off, although this particular weather no longer bothered Willian as much as it had used to when he had resembled a human-being. Each and every rain droplet now slid from Willian's scaly hide with ease. Still, Willian couldn't help feeling that he would still much rather be shivering uncontrollably and soaked right through if it meant he could be a human again, rather than this horrific and evil mix between blessed human and cursed demon-spawn.

A distinctive aroma of human assailed Willian's nostrils at the very same time that he made out the sound of small feet clumsily making their way in his direction through the darkness. He quickly scampered up the wide trunk of the ancient tree that he had been leaning against a moment ago with his new-found webbed talons and concealed himself within the dripping; leafy boughs, watching and waiting in fervent hope that this traveller would be that son of a cur, Everhart Bovenwater. Although something about the scent seemed off to Willian.

However, his twisted hopes were quickly dashed when the slender figure of a woman stalked past his advantageous lookout post, cursing as she tripped over on overturned rocks hidden in the shadows. Willian hastily blinked his Decona eyes in the night darkness and tried to make out some more details of this single, unassuming human, as it was the first he had seen in his entire journey chasing Everhart and his seer. Human-being's appeared to be scarce in these parts. The lone woman carried a magnificent bow and quiver of arrows upon her back, far too noble to belong to a girl such as this. She must have stolen it, thought Willian as an explanation to himself - only men were deserving of weapons such as that cunningly crafted article. The beautiful bow seemed to sing to Willian and soothe his deformed soul for no reason that he could explain to himself. He felt in his heart that the bow would fit his scaled, webbed hands perfectly, although the bow and arrows had never been his weapon of choice previously. As a human, Willian had preferred a weapon of dexterity such as a dagger to match his cunning nature, something that you could feel sticking in to someone as you used it.

His improved sense of smell and keen vision also told Willian that the female was carrying three or four freshly killed rabbits at her belt. An excessive amount for one woman surely thought Willian? She must be travelling with others and not too far away. The women must have gone to get food for her group. The thought of food made Willian salivate hungrily as his belly grumbled in protest at its continued emptiness. He patted his belly encouragingly, promising it that when he had his hands on the seer it would be fed the most luxurious foods in the land. Then ignoring his hunger pangs, Willian hesitantly leaned further out on a sturdy branch and gazed intently at the girl who was slowly striding out of his view. She lifted a small bony hand and flicked back her sleek, dark, dripping hair from her face and Willian's heart leapt with recognition. It was Vita! Surely if she was here collecting provisions for more than one person it could mean only one thing. Everhart and the seer must be close too!

Willian leapt recklessly from the damp tree and landed perfectly on the balls of his feet on the sodden earth. He skulked after Vita at a safe distance, not wanting to reveal himself yet and prayed that she would lead him to his salvation and Everhart's deserved demise.

14

Pzzztttt! A miniscule, electric blue spark flickered erratically and danced awkwardly across Everhart's knuckles briefly and then extinguished itself abruptly leaving a faint burnt smell tainting the cool night air, reminding Everhart of the stench created when wax candles were blown out.

"Pah! I'll never master this elemental nonsense," spat Everhart disheartened at his poor performance, "I can hardly protect Loki against anything if my magic only amounts to parlour tricks now can I! What am I supposed to do with that little spark, entertain at a wealthy toddler's Birthday celebration? It's too unpredictable Mopsus!"

Mopsus shook his grey muzzled head indulgently at the petulant and quick tempered outburst and tutted at Everhart with a wry smile upon his whiskered face, "My dear friend, we haven't even been practicing this particular method for half an hour yet and you have already made substantial and impressive progress. More than I have ever seen from a new learner in such a short period of time. Do you know how many years it takes a Knight in ordinary circumstances to learn to use his magic effectively? And that tutoring usually begins from early childhood - you are obviously disadvantaged as you have grown up without this regular guidance. Nevertheless, you are now beginning to make use of a power that even this very morning you didn't even realise you had. Be content child and do away with this impatient nature so we can get on with making some progress!"

Loki could not resist grinning a white, toothy grin at his grey-muzzled double and he rolled his sparkling eyes in an exaggerated manner that was for Everhart's benefit entirely. "He is always like this unfortunately Mopsus," confided the younger tiger in an overly loud tone that was obviously meant for his friend Everhart to hear with ease, "Lord knows what he would be like if he did not have me around to drag him out of his sour moods all the time!"

The elderly tiger smiled back at the good natured teasing, and the scowl that perpetrated Everhart's face, which clearly showed the deep reaching bond between the two individuals. "Indeed. You two are the most elegant balancing act that I could have ever dreamt up. A court conjurer would have severe competition with you two in the vicinity. The unbreakable bond that you two share will serve you well in your long lives." Mopsus then turned abruptly to face Everhart solely, "Now, Master Everhart, I counsel you to take a short break and then perhaps we can work on your use of heat and fire. I know you are intent on learning to master the elegant fury of lightning but I feel that fire would match your strong passion and suit your temperament much more. In my day, most Knights excelled on one elemental area in particular, although they could control all of them to a certain extent with time of course. The elements that they could control best more often than not complemented their personality and temperament. Lightning went to the more judgmental sorts who were unlikely to wait around, water to the ones with unpredictable actions, fire to the more spirited with a burning passion..."

Everhart sighed heavily, smoothing his hair back absent-mindedly and nodded at Mopsus, more out of respect for the ancient creature of legend than in any true sign of any sort of agreement to the comment.

"Tell me then Mopsus, if my question isn't too bold," gestured Everhart with a pointed finger, tipped with a roughly bitten fingernail, "where are these supposed Knights that you speak of? And where is the race of the Soothsayers? Are we the only ones that remain of our kinds? For surely if the tales you have told us this evening are true then you should have your own Knight here to protect you with elemental magic, yet none has stood in our path or revealed himself to us and I find it difficult to digest that our species is actually more common than we know when we have never discovered another like us before yourself?"

Mopsus let out a heart-breaking, pained and lengthy sigh at the barrage of questions from his newly acquired pupil and motioned with his head for his new acquaintances to join him once more in sitting around the fire that had now begun to die down to glowing embers. As he did so, a rather soggy Vita arrived at the cave entrance with a multitude of sodden fur attached to her leather belt. She shook herself, almost like a pet dog clambering out of a lake and patches of rainwater splattered into the dryness of the cave that the stormy weather had failed to reach.

"Vita!" crowed Loki with genuine joy in his deep voice, "Come and warm yourself by the fireside my wily girl. You look like you need it more than us and you're just in time for a story from Mopsus here by the seems of it."

Although visibly still intensely agitated that she didn't fit in as much as the others, Vita had quickly come to love Loki's kind, positive attitude and merry nature and responded to it without thought, so she automatically found herself sitting down by the fireside without question and she habitually began to skin the deceased rabbits and clean them out methodically ready to cook. Mopsus wrinkled his black, wet nose distastefully at the messy and smelly task which immediately made Loki grin with pleasure.

"Do you avoid eating meat also then my friend?" Loki asked inquisitively, "For I've never had a liking for the stuff either, much to Everhart's amusement. He seemed to assume that I should be a natural predator as a big cat and hunt everything down with tooth and claw when we first met, but he quickly became accustomed to my taste for fruits and roots in the time since we have been together and his skills at whipping up a mini feast for a large vegetarian are not to be sniffed at. Even the simple thought of such an act as putting another creature's flesh in my mouth makes me feel nauseous."

"It is normal for us to behave this way Loki and your tastes are not an aberration for our species. No Soothsayer that I know of hunts and consumes flesh, Loki my fast becoming friend. And usually no Knight either for that matter. Although I think as Everhart's mastery of his powers grows, his taste for meat will diminish in kind. It is the correct balance. No one should possess that amount of power along with a desire to use such immense power to the detriment of others. However, I am not of the mind of berating others. Convince not condemn is my motto."

Vita's slender jaw hung open and her eyes darted between the others at the fire before a mischievous grin enlightened her clammy face that was still cold and damp from the outside rain, "Everhart!? Powers!" she throatily laughed incredulously, "I've evidently been away hunting for far longer than I had realised. I go off for a brief hunting trip and when I return you have whipped up severe illusions of grandeur for yourself! Maybe you are delusional from lack of food Everhart. Never fear, I'll have these rabbits over the fire and your grumbling belly filled before you know it my poor friend."

Everhart shot her an indignant glare, affronted and upset at her surprise and mocking particularly since he was disappointed in himself for not being able to utilise the Knight's magic as effectively as he thought he should be able, but Vita just laughed it off playfully, not noticing that she had dented her friend's pride, as usual. It wasn't difficult to see that she and Everhart had severe issues in interpreting the actions and the reactions that the other displayed. Mopsus had already noted as much in his head.

"Anyway, I didn't forget about you two." She advised kindly, pulling a bundle of juicy, yet bruised and wet apples and some light roots out of her sodden haversack. "You want to try these roasted over the fire to warm up your insides. Not bad, even for my carnivorous tastes I'll have you know. You ought to try it mixed with some hummus and a sprinkling of pepper between two slices of fresh bread just cooled from the oven, not that I have any of that to hand just at the minute mind you - I struggled to happen across a baker's establishment at this time of night in the current area."

Mopsus thanked Vita gravely, realising that this was the first thing that another living being had done for him in a very long time. Small acts of kindness that expected nothing in return made the world the wonderful and inspiring place that it was to him and every time an atrocious act damaged his heart almost to breaking point he could recall a time that his heart had almost burst with joy at some happy and carefree action witnessed by himself. Loki simply gave Vita a whiskery nudge under her cold chin with his large head in thanks before turning to the elderly tiger excitedly.

"So, Mopsus. Where exactly is the rest of our kind? I would

love to meet others like ourselves for, as I have said, I have not had the chance to meet any, sparing yourself of course. We truly thought that I was just a unique aberration."

"In short dear Loki, the stark truth is that I truly don't know for certain. We were chased here, to this spot, long ago, longer than I care to remember, after we had set out to follow a vision from our leading seer. It was vitally important, yet some people often hold messenger's responsible for something that is no fault of their own, thinking they will cause the visions that they have to become reality, rather than trying to stop then and steer the future onto a safer path for all. We vowed not to hurt anyone if we could help it, even the vicious group that had given us chase, and so the seers and the Knights retreated instead. I was elderly even at that time for a seer and I soon realised that I was slowing the others down. My Knight...he...he was cut down by the delirious mob on our way here, when we were much behind our group, having stayed behind to protect me. He was too distracted by my weary state to realise what was happening until it was too late. He was already gone and so I begged the others to go on without me and implored them to cut the bridge after they had crossed in order to slow the mob down. I thought that they would find me in truth and their torment of me would slow them down further but they never found this cave or me safe inside it. I think they must have lost interest when their tempers and fears had calmed.

You may have seen the remains of the ancient bridge that was cut down on your way to me. I prefer not to look at it anymore. It holds troublesome memories for me. I've never seen any of the seers or Knights since that fateful day, neither in reality nor in one of my visions. I thought once that if they were no more, then I would feel it but...as time lengthened with no contact, I thought, who knows what the truth may be. Maybe they are truly gone forever more, but maybe they managed to prevent the occurrence in the vision and begin a new home?"

Silence descended upon the group after those melancholy words, as each person sat around the fire pondered the tale and what it meant for them. The only sound that could be heard was the rhythmic dripping of cool rain drops from the dew laden trees that surrounded the relative haven of the cave. Loki truly wanted to know more of that day in detail. Did the mob find another way to follow the seers and the Knights? How did Mopsus manage to remain unnoticed and unscathed in this simple cave? What had happened to Mopsus after the death of his beloved Knight and who had he been? Everhart wanted to know the answers to these important questions also but neither wanted to ask them at the cost of unearthing many years of lonely hurt in their new found friend Mopsus.

Vita was still somewhat lacking, if not in empathy, then at least in the sympathetic tact that Everhart and Loki possessed and demonstrated.

"Human mob!?" she queried in an angered shrill voice that did nothing to mask the fury in it, "Why, is that how you see all of us humans then tiger?! As an unruly mob not as talented as yourselves? I assure you that not all of us are intent on hunting your kind to extinction! I've spent all this time doing my utmost to protect Loki...and Everhart!"

"And you will protect them to your end girl," spoke Mopsus cryptically, "but know that at this present time in this world, those like yourself are few and far between, although I would imagine that they may have a quick temper to match that of yourself. There are more out there than you know akin to those of that horde of aggressive humans, who would have no reservations over hunting us down under the false impression that we can grant to them other-worldly powers and glory and can turn them into whatever it is that they wish to be. They will cut down all those in between them and us as well, including other humans without a glimmer of remorse or a moment's hesitation! Unfortunately this power that they imagine we can grant unto them is simply untrue and beyond any seer's capability that I am aware of. Our visions can help other's make decisions but that is all."

Now truly offended, without a smile or a wink, Mopsus rose from the warmth of the glowing fire and silently padded on wide spreading paws to face the mossy wall at the far end of the cold cave. Everhart shot Vita a baleful glare in rebuke at her unkind words and moved over to join Mopsus and to offer yet another apology on behalf of his loyal yet irksome friend Vita. Loki rose and loyally followed Everhart as he always did in times of unrest. Vita found herself alone at the edge of a dying fire.

15

Willian had carefully and silently followed Vita all the way back to the cave that was obviously functioning as the runaway's hideout. He had cleverly managed to conceal himself close to the entrance of the cave within the cover of the night shadows of the swaying trees, and although his human ears had now shrivelled away to practically nothing, his hearing was now so keen that if he concentrated hard enough, he could pick up every individual word that was being uttered within the shelter of the cavernous dwelling. At first he was shocked and horrified to discover that yet another feline abomination existed within the modern world, also talking as if it were a righteous being, yet then his morale heightened swiftly as he imagined how much precious power and influence he would wield, back as a human in his rightful form, and with not one, but two magical beasts at his command. His thin lipless face spread in an eerie smile. That was of course, until the decrepit beast had uttered that last damning sentence, crushing his hopes and ambitions in one fell swoop!

"Noooooooooooooooooooo!!!" he howled in acute agony, his chest feeling as if it had been crushed, making it difficult to draw a breath, and dashed forward into the gloom of the cave, baying for the blood and death of all.

*****

The wild, agonised, howl from outside drew everyone in the cave's attention immediately. Everhart lifted his head to see a small, malformed Decona bounding speedily into the cave and brandishing some sort of crude, makeshift, flint blade, heading with crazed eyes full of bloodlust towards a confused Loki who seemed to be frozen for the moment. Everhart raised his clenched fist to the roof of the cave and dramatically flung his arm outwards towards the intruder, begging his new power to destroy this imminent threat in a storm of lightening. A tiny fizzling noise sounded and one, solitary, small spark danced briefly across Everhart's knuckle before extinguishing into nothingness. Nothing else happened and the delay in his attempt at magic meant that the crazed Decona was nearly on top of Loki. Everhart's chest tightened fearfully as he lurched forward, knowing he would never make it to the other half of his heart in time now. He had squandered his chance to rescue him.

A strong feminine shout sounded from Vita's mouth as she flung herself bodily without reservation in between Loki and the oncoming deranged Decona. She had intended to bring the creature down and pin him to the ground, yet the creature's body and the make-shift blade he clutched twisted unexpectedly with the force of her jump and embedded itself in the exposed side of her soft, pale neck as, a second too late, Mopsus landed perfectly on the attacker and snapped his spine with one powerful swipe of his forepaw and an audible crack.

"Nooo...Vita!" bellowed Everhart in despair, reaching the melee and scooping Vita's weightless body up effortlessly to cradle her in his powerful arms, ignoring the crumpled corpse of the attacker that was now twitching randomly by his booted feet. Violent spurts of thick, scarlet blood pushed carelessly out of the sleek wound in Vita's neck, coating Everhart's arms and hands in its shocking slickness. So much blood, thought Everhart, heartbroken in the knowledge that this situation could not be righted. Vita just gazed into Everhart's big, bright, tear-brimming eyes and smiled a sleepy smile at him, as she opened her mouth slowly to try and speak.

"I love those big, green eyes of yours," she breathed out shallowly, a slither of blood meandering down from the corner of her lip, "tell Loki I said to look after them Ever…" She sighed contently and closed her own eyes, her slight hand relaxed releasing the sparkling arrow that she had been clutching and that she had decided she didn't have time to notch if she was to save the life of Loki.

Everhart buried his face unashamedly into the front of her blood soaked jerkin that was still sodden from the downpour she had wandered off in to supply the evening's dinner. As Everhart sobbed brokenly into her chest, his companion let out her final breath easily. Loki and Mopsus looked on silently in shocked horror and bowed their heads respectfully.

*****

Everhart sat sorrowfully next to the fresh grave that was now the final resting place of the body of a friend who had left everything she had known to follow Loki and himself. She was someone who had given all she had, despite thinking that she would get nothing in return. The morning sun shone fiercely down upon Everhart, drying the moist mud on top of Vita's grave, next to the opening of the cave in which she had breathed her last breath. Everhart had picked a solitary, pale, lily that had been growing close by. The flower of death was as lovely in its simplicity as Vita had been.

Mopsus motioned to Loki with a nod of his head, to follow him and leave his friend to grieve and come to terms with his loss and also with his guilt that he had needlessly assumed. The two tigers walked in silence a goodly distance from Everhart and then sat leisurely on their haunches, warming their fur in the baking heat of the morning sun.

"I think I knew that something like this would happen," Loki confided to Mopsus sorrowfully, his voice tainted with guilt, "I just had a feeling. Not exactly a vision, but more than a gut feeling.

Words of foreboding kept entering my mind and falling out of my mouth. I should have told someone what I thought it mean..."

"Most seers experience that Loki, but just sharing that knowledge isn't always enough to avert a disaster. I had the same sensation about that girl the moment she ran into my home last night and I first laid eyes on her. Everhart should use this painful incident as a harsh lesson to realise not to throw himself headlong into things and just expect everything to turn out alright, although at the same time, you pair cannot keep collecting guilt that does not belong to you."

"You can't say this was Ever's fault!" argued an indignant Loki, fur bristling in anger, "He can't even use his powers yet and that is through no fault of our own either! His parents left Aither without telling us anything of what he was, and ... I cannot even remember the slightest thing about my own parents or how I came to be in Aither's woodland!"

Mopsus nodded his large head more in acknowledgement than agreement, "All the same Loki, if Everhart was not always so impatient with himself to master his powers immediately, then perhaps he would decide to take a different course of action on occasion and if you weren't so defensive of your friend you would see his impatience more clearly. Did you not yourself laugh and joke of it last night when the situation was not so fraught? What the two of you need to realise young one, is that these powers and awe-inspiring abilities are a part of you only, not the whole of each of you. Everhart is not just a protector and you are not just a seer. And in regards to both sets of your parents, perhaps they will yet have something to teach you."

Loki leapt up placing a huge paw on each of Mopsus' grey shoulders, and his enchanting eyes stared imploring into the eyes of the other tiger.

"Do you know something of our parent's then? Please tell me Mopsus!" he begged hopefully.

"Of your own parents, all I can say is that for two seers lines to be cut so short at the same time would be a rare and powerful occurrence, and like with those of our kind who fled, I think that I should have felt something like that happen. How you came to be alone in the woods without their aid is a mystery to me and a tale yet to be uncovered. But, as for Everhart's parents, I am unsure, but I did dream of two humans who had travelled in search of the seers to ask about their emerald-eyed son. They arrived safely and received the information that they required. In my visions, those two did not perish but remained with their hosts for reasons that are unclear to me at this time."

Loki let out a deep, exuberant whoop! "This will lift Ever's spirits some and give him hope! Thank you Mopsus my friend!" With that Loki twisted his graceful body with ease and galloped at break-neck speed back towards his Knight, Everhart, yelling triumphantly, "Everhart! Your parents! They might yet still be alive my friend!"

16

Mopsus wisely gave the two friends a bit of time on their own to sort through their mixed up feelings at the last few weeks events, before he headed down to join them. The pair slumped against each other, emerald eyes open and teary, staring up at the clear sky.

"So my friends," he asked gently, "where will you head now may I ask, for I am afraid that I cannot give you any help as in to which direction your path may lie and any visions I may have after you are gone will obviously be of no help to you then?"

Loki heaved himself up from the ground, reluctant to leave the warmth of his friend but curious enough to do so. He cocked his head to one side inquisitively as he addressed the other seer.

"Well, why aren't you coming with us Mopsus" he queried in a genuinely confused tone.

"There truly is no need for you to stay here alone friend," joined in Everhart sincerely, "I know that I can be a bit short tempered on occasion and I realise I failed catastrophically last night and for that alone I can never be truly forgiven, but I am certain that I can protect you now, and in truth I would feel better knowing that you had some company. Besides, in all honesty, I still could do with your guidance in learning how to use my powers correctly."

"My place is no longer in the middle of things I am afraid, Sir

Knight. Although, the gallant offer of yours is very thoughtful and reassures me that the world is in the hands of a modest and kind heart. Unfortunately, I feel my time on this plane is growing short and I would rather spend my last days curled up in sublime peace in familiar surroundings rather than uprooting myself to go on some unending journey. Unfortunately, I have to admit that I am incredibly old, even for one of my kind, and I am beginning to feel it now more than ever. And now that I have met you two youngsters and I can be sure that you do exist, I feel my purpose has been fulfilled" To emphasise this point Mopsus stretched out, digging his claws into the earth and lifting up his back end where small popping noises could be heard from his aching back, "Of course I shall be more than happy to tutor you until you and Loki decide to leave however."

Everhart looked somewhat disappointed and struggled to hide it. "But, I can't leave you here to fend for yourself," a mournful smile ghosted across his chapped lips as he nervously bit his bottom lip, tearing a flake of dry skin off, "I wouldn't have heard the end of it from Vita you know. She was somewhat persistent in letting me know how I should be looking after people. Isn't there anything at all that I can do for you?" A sad smile sat upon Everhart's face and Mopsus felt the need to humour Everhart and ease the suffering slightly of this honourable soul by giving him something to do to make himself feel useful.

"Well, as I said, I am getting on in years son, and moving heavy weights really does irk my aching back for days afterwards." Mopsus again stretched his front paws forward theatrically, emitting another sharp, cracking noise from his back, although this hadn't seemed to hinder him much when he had launched himself at the attacking Decona previously, thought Loki suspiciously, catching on quickly to Mopsus' plan.

Everhart's spirit appeared to brighten marginally, "What can I move for you then old man?" he asked impishly, flexing his young muscles in a display intended to impress and amuse Mopsus in equal measure.

"Well..." the elderly tiger paused, suddenly realising his well-meant request might not turn out to be quite an appropriate gesture to take Everhart's mind off his sorrow, "That body is still in my home..." he glanced up towards the cave.

A grim, intimidating look washed across Everhart's flushed face and without a further word he stalked stiffly into the cave without a further word. Loki quickly followed his friend towards the cave and Mopsus trailed behind starting to regret his good intentions and silently cursing himself for not thinking things through. All three stood looking down on the stiff, cooled corpse for a moment, reflecting on their individual thoughts and feelings that seemed to have been raked mercilessly over the coals in the last twenty-four hours.

Everhart let out a deep, pained sigh, "I just don't understand it," he uttered in a sorrowful murmur, truly at a loss to explain the situation to himself, "why would a Decona suddenly attack us with no provocation. I thought that we had formed some sort of loose alliance with them after we guested in their underground home and they gifted us with these marvellous weapons that seemed worthy of royalty rather than us to me." His hand smoothed down the length of his lethal yet handsome broadsword and he heaved up the beautiful quiver of arrows and curved bow that he now wore upon his muscled back, that had recently belonged to his wonderful and infuriating friend Vita. His sighs were interrupted by Loki, who flicked his tail in the air - still fitted with the deadly contraption that he had been gifted with by the Decona, which was something that he also had not managed to utilise to save Vita from her unfair fate.

"Me too Everhart," he said softly, "I thought they gave these things to us as a sign of friendship and for us to make use of to protect ourselves and others?"

"As indeed they did," interrupted Mopsus, "knowing you were worthy and important beings in the folds of time they intended for you to use these weapons, yet neither of you did. You must both realise that you must use any tool you have in your reach to protect others if the good in the world is to survive. You both had impressive weapons in your possession, yet nevertheless, you were both so caught up in the realisation of your legendary gifts that they were all you attempted to use. You must be patient in mastering them and when you have done this still realise that they may not always be the best option. You must also realise that now you have them, it will not be an easy journey. There are those that will hate you for them and try to take them away from you. It is a difficult balancing act indeed."

Loki hung his head down in shame, yet recent events meant that Everhart didn't need much of an excuse to get irritable and he wasn't quite as sensible as Loki when it came to controlling his feelings.

"That's all well and good!" he snapped in fury, "But that has nothing to do with why this damn Decona attacked us in the first place and killed our friend, Vita!"

"Oh dear," Mopsus said whilst sniffing at the scaly body with disdain, "I truly have been living alone for too long. I have forgotten that everyone does not know what I know and cannot sense all I can. Everhart my friend, this corpse at your feet is not that of a Decona."

Everhart shot his hands to his hips, in a sad parody of Vita.

"What are you harping on about Mopsus? Did you take a knock to the head taking down this filthy beast for I have eyes and I can see what this is?"

It appeared almost impossible for Everhart to offend the old tiger, who merely smiled at Everhart's rude retort and good naturedly began to explain his statement.

"As a seer, when we are in contact with a living being, it is possible for us to have flashes of knowledge of that being. This is what makes it possible for us to do what we call a reading. The older we are and the more years we have spent on this plane, then the more information comes to us in these flashes about someone, and the contact needn't be for a lengthy period. Consequently, when I pounced on this pitiful creature, I knew him implicitly. He was a vile beast that murdered an innocent Decona child and drank his warm blood in the expectation that he would gain all the knowledge of the Decona as the legends tell. What he didn't realise was that passing on memories in this specific manner and the blood dreams that ensue are only intended for the Decona. The Decona blood itself knew this, and so it has done its best to ensure that the host became as Decona as it possibly could. However, this cowardly body could not support the immense transformation. He knew he was not right inside and he was under the mistaken impression that a seer could reverse this mutation."

Everhart bent down to the body and prodded its scaled cheek experimentally with his outstretched finger.

"What was it then? Originally I mean?" he mused.

"He was a human, an ordinary one, like your Vita," answered Mopsus knowingly, "not a very good example of one as she was, in my humble opinion, but a human nonetheless. He was from your quiet village of Aither and he followed you, suspecting you 'had' a seer. His name was Willian Liew."

As Mopsus had been talking, Everhart's large hands had balled themselves into angry fists so tight that his knuckles became a deathly white and the veins stuck out like blue worms under his stretched skin. At the mention of the name, Everhart let out a roar loud enough to match that of a pained tiger.

"Why when he knew Vita and I for most of our lives and we never did him any harm! Why!!"

With his outburst, Everhart flung his arms out accusingly at the corpse and in response a string of searing flames sprang from his hands and engulfed Willian's malformed body in their light. The crackling heat was so oppressive and it grew at such a speed that the three companions had to make a hasty retreat from the cave in order to protect themselves from injury.

Everhart's green eyes were wide as he attempted to comprehend what he had just done, whilst Loki seemed more concerned for his friend than impressed by the fiery destruction and was rubbing around his legs almost like a tame house cat. Surprisingly, Mopsus let out a throaty bark that served as his laugh at the situation.

"Well, it seems that you won't need my help Knight. The most powerful seer and knight duo that have ever been seen have arrived."

17

"The Unfortunates will be the doom of this world if their progress is not impeded." announced Calogero chilling.

To his right, his Knight, Latasha dutifully recorded the prominent words in an elaborately, leather bound book with an extravagant inked quill fashioned from a single, bright, peacock feather. The Knight remained silent as was usual and did not ask any questions. If Calogero had spoken no other words then he knew nothing else to add to the account. Calogero was insistent on recording everything word for word in case the visions needed to be looked over at a later date.

Latasha thought that most of the world was unfortunate these days, and so she had no idea which unfortunate's in particular Calogero's vision alluded to. From the irritated grimace on Calogero's face, it appeared that neither did he.

Calogero was the biggest and most intimidating seer that Latasha had ever seen in her days as a Knight. Even on all fours, she estimated that the tiger stood at least four feet off the ground, and if he stood on his striped hind legs he was simply overwhelmingly. This was fitting, being as he was nominally considered to be the rightful leader of the remaining seers and the Knights. His rich fur was sleek and more orangey-brown than the other seers, with his black stripes so dark that they looked as if they could swallow you whole. The looming tiger had no mate. Even Latasha had to admit that he wasn't one for sympathy and showing any vulnerability that he may possess. Not that he was unnecessarily cruel by any measures, but he was strict, stern and he took his role as leader incredibly seriously. His personality being this way inclined, Calogero had refused to take a mate, stating that it was completely unnecessary being as the seers no longer seemed to be able to breed and produce new life anyway.

Latasha had never been privileged enough to witness a new seer or Knight being born and she was now approaching her mid-forties, as was her ward Calogero. Calogero knew it was a serious problem that impinged on the future of their kind, but he didn't often speak of it, although Latasha was certain it was always on his mind. Calogero's father stoutly refused to speak of it when he was alive either, although Latasha always thought that the old tiger had had a theory behind the problem from the manner in which he avoided any questioning on the matter. When the old tiger suddenly died seven years ago from a freak accident, along with Calogero's mother, Latasha had felt devastated and sure that an opportunity to uncover and fix the dooming problem had been lost, forcing her to cruelly watch her race slowly die out.

The Knight had no mate either, although there was no real reason why she shouldn't have one. She was a striking woman even with fifty creeping up on her. She was tall, slender and well-muscled with a flat belly, but in a pleasant, rather than a daunting way. Her hair was still mostly dark brown with only a few thin, grey hairs dotted here and there, and it was as long as a fabled maidens and she always wore it in a practical braid which swung down past her waist and was always bound with a simple, leather thong. Her eyelashes were incredibly long and curled out atop her huge emerald eyes, which along with her prominent cheekbones made her look thoroughly at home with the big cats that were her family.

"I've made a note of your words." advised Latasha as she gently closed the pages of the book together and placed it softly to the side of her.

"For what it's worth," Calogero sneered in an uncharacteristically sour manner, "I know, Latasha, that this is the most important message that I have ever had the misfortune of pronouncing. But I do not understand it. The vision accompanying it is so dark and terrible that I cannot see it clearly. Yet, I know with all my soul that if we fail to get to the bottom of it, the world will be doomed and the end will be near for us. This problem is the most vitally important matter that we have ever faced by far and must be resolved with haste."

Calogero was making Latasha incredibly nervous. Rambling and despairing was not usually his cool style. She attempted to distract him from his dark thoughts and return his musings to other important matters at hand.

"The most important matter that we have faced? Surely Calogero, it cannot be as important as the dwindling of our race. Should that not be addressed first? For what is the purpose of saving our kind from this darkness you speak of, only to have us dwindle and die out not decades after?"

She had anticipated an angry response from her friend and leader, for with all of his reserve and coolness he was still that, and a bit of debate over how he had thought that particular problem through again and again, but he still managed to surprise her.

"If we do not solve this hellish problem, Latasha, then our dwindling race will be irrelevant," said Calogero seriously, "when I say the world will be doomed, I mean it."

18

He opened his dry eyes suddenly and an insatiable hunger immediately hit him with its full force. If he hadn't already been lying down, he feared it would have driven him to his knees with sheer shock at its ferocious intensity. The first sensible realisation after this was that he was covered in a fair amount of jagged shale and pebbles, completely buried in the unforgiving ground, yet it seemed to have no impact on his ability to breathe. Digging himself out of the shallow grave with his slender arms was no effort at all and this led him to his second realisation. He was now strong, more than simply strong and he was perfectly formed. He stretched his long arms out in front of his eyes and focused on them intently. He seemed to vaguely recall that they had been painfully crooked and deformed once before, as had his legs. But this was not the case anymore. His long limbs were still slight and lithe, devoid of much evident muscle but possessing unnatural and immense strength all the same. He fervently tried to recall how it was that he had gotten to this point, but all he could recall was drinking the most enriching substance that he had ever had the pleasure to consume, blood. He wanted more of it. He knew he needed more of it, nothing else seemed to matter in comparison and the thought alone made him salivate hungrily, encouraging stringy saliva to congregate at the edges of his thin lips. He swallowed longingly and moved his wet tongue in his mouth, only to discover that he now seemed to possess a killer set of perfectly formed fangs. He used his tongue and fingers to investigate the new discovery further. The fangs had replaced the third tooth on his upper set of teeth on either side of his mouth. They were thick and deadly sharp, protruding so long that with his mouth closed they jutted out over his thin upper lip, but not uncomfortably as one might expect. They felt as if that was where they belonged. He knew he definitely did not possess these spectacular fangs before. However, he didn't seem to know a lot else at all, not even about himself. What was his name for instance he thought? He pondered this for a while and found that the only thing that stuck out in his mind was the phrase "The Unfortunate". He wasn't sure if it was truly a name but it was all he had and it sounded familiar to him.

"The Unfortunate." he said out loud to test how the words sounded upon his lips. His voice crackled like a spitting, burning log upon a burning fire. It sounded raspy, cruel and severely out of practice. In fact, he mused to himself, he couldn't remember when he had last utilised his voice, or if in fact he had ever spoken with it at all. He didn't utter anything else after this though, as his hunger was becoming so urgent and insistent that it was beginning to impede on his every waking thought. He decided that he needed to address it immediately and then he would have the ability to ponder other avenues. He could scarcely think clearly if he did not deal with the ravenous feeling growing in his stomach. He scanned the distant horizon keenly. It appeared to be night-time, something he had only just realised, so absorbed had he been in discovering the new aspects of himself, nevertheless, he felt incredibly alert and fully awake and he could see more clearly than he ever could recall having done so before. He grinned, widely enough that his new found fangs grazed the top of his bottom lip, releasing a smear of fluid and he immediately took off running, faster than a hunting cheetah with no effort what-so-ever.

The tantalising smell of a hundred different unknown scents danced on the night breeze and he revelled in them all as they twisted through his flaring nostrils and into his expanding lungs. He breathed them all in as deeply as he could, his chest expanding pleasurably, whilst searching for one that he could identify as sustenance that would satisfy this ravenous and merciless hunger. He wasn't sure how long he had been running, without ever slowing down, when an inviting aroma invaded his nostrils and caught his bare feet skidding to a sudden halt. Looking around, he seemed to have come to the muddy outskirts of a sleepy village. A village that he thought he may have been to before. All was deathly quiet, and it appeared few were up, apart from the baker making the morning's bread by the look of the thick smoke that curled lazily from one lone chimney.

"Aither." he rasped knowingly.

"Huh," a sole slurred voice asked querulously from just outside the village fence, evidently hearing his utterance, "who be there?" The voice was incoherently slurred with alcohol and it sounded more confused than scared. Evidently it was someone trying to make their way home from the Inn and struggling to find the correct direction after consuming one too many drinks. An unlooked for thought told him that he had once followed someone else in a similar situation after feeling an unexplainable and inexplicable dark bond to them. The stray thought surprised him, but he didn't allow it to distract him from his goal.

He was behind the human in a blink of a mortal eye, his exaggerated speed still surprising even himself much to his pleasure.

"An Unfortunate," he croaked in answer to the question, still getting used to the sound of his own voice, "somewhat like you."

The Unfortunate gripped the drunken sot's shoulder's with an inescapable iron grip, his slender fingers digging in roughly and drawing blood as he instinctively sank his sharp fangs into the man's slightly flabby neck. His senses were so keen that he could smell the man's sour stench of cold sweat that was finally filled with the aroma of primal fear and he almost fancied that he felt the teeth penetrate a few, distasteful, layers of unneeded fat before the luscious, thick, warm blood filled his mouth with the most glorious taste imaginable. He gulped it down greedily as the human's whimpering and struggling got weaker and weaker before failing altogether. When he had eventually had his full and felt satiated, and before he had drained the human to uselessness, he ceased sucking the blood through the wounds that he had made and heaved the, now still, body over his left shoulder, carrying it off with him with ease. He had the feeling it was the right thing to do and the start of something new.

19

The Unfortunate had been absolutely fascinated whilst watching the transformation of his captive, wondering if this was the same thing that had happened to him before he awoke to his absorbing new life. At first the drained human's breathing and heartbeat had gotten quieter and quieter until they had ceased completely. This was all that happened for a few moments and so The Unfortunate had thought at first that he had taken too much blood from his victim and killed the human. With a mental shrug he had been prepared to leave it at that and curl up and hide from the light of the day upon the simple, abandoned bed that took up most of this disused and run-down shed of a cottage that he had decided to stop in, when the dawn had risen and he realised that the bright, morning light assailed his sensitive eyes and become quickly unbearable.

However, at that moment the creature's eyes had suddenly shot open. And such magnificent eyes they were! When he had sunk his fangs into the flabby neck of the human last night, the man's eyes had been a dirty, dull brown, as like to horse dung as could be, although quite bloodshot due to the amount of alcohol present in his system, but now they were utterly astounding. There was no clear pupil defined and eye white as you would expect to see in an ordinary creature's eye, but instead the entire eye was a perfect inky black. So dark were they that the almost looked like two dark holes into which you could trip and be swallowed into the cruel abyss below. The Unfortunate hoped and wondered whether his eyes were the same as that, as he hadn't managed to see his reflection since he had awoken and had no idea what features now graced his newly awoken face.

The once-human creature had then begun to shake with violent convulsions whilst rich, red, blood spewed from its mouth and bubbled from its flaring nostrils. It writhed around the dusty, wooden, floor smearing blood in with the dirt whilst its limbs thrashed wildly around making distinct cracking sounds as if they were being broken and moulded into something anew altogether. This went on for a number of hours that were no doubt distinctly painful for the transformed if the screaming was anything to go by, before the transformation seemed to be complete. After the creature had been reborn it spent a further hour or more silent and still with its captivating eyes closed to the world again.

The Unfortunate was almost agitated with excitement as he eagerly anticipated what would happen next to his new creature, and took to cleaning his nails, which were now, long, black, pointed and animal like, with this shining, white, teeth whilst he waited for it to awaken. His eyes glanced to the still and bloody corpse after each nail was cleaned to check that he had not missed any change.

Its black eyes eventually opened soundlessly and it rose to its feet with elegant ease, oblivious to the hours of pain that he had previously endured in such a horrific manner. The creature then performed a subservient bow that seemed out of sorts with the haphazard human that The Unfortunate has happened upon outside the village of Aither.

"Who am I?" asked the creature blankly once it had risen out if its bow.

The Unfortunate grinned wickedly with pleasure as this fortunate occurrence of events.

"You are an Unfortunate," he answered "as am I. I am the one who gave you this life."

The new born creature nodded his pale head and accepted this answer without further question.

"I will follow you," the new born creature stated, bowing its head subserviently.

Now this was an intriguing notion thought The Original Unfortunate. Someone that he had once known would have said that he now possessed 'a freak on a leash'.

"Are you hungry?" queried The Original Unfortunate.

"Ravenous," was the quick reply.

20

Calogero's warning visions involving the word 'unfortunate' and not much else, had seemed to multiply and become more and more urgent over the last few days, although they did not seen to provide any new information that could be used to their advantage. Latasha had started to become increasingly concerned and the worrying ensured that severe headaches now plagued her. She pushed the knuckle of her forefinger on her left hand into her temple in an attempt to dull the irritating pain as she assessed the situation on her mind. Her seer rarely had a vision with the same topic more than a handful of times. This intensity of visions had never happened before and was becoming serious.

So serious in fact, that Calogero had called a formal meeting, summoning the remaining seers and Knights. Latasha could not recall such a meeting ever being called previously in her time. If it had done, she must have been just a babe in arms. Calogero's father had occasionally spoken to him of the meeting he had called when the decision had been made to leave the world of human's behind, but no other decisions had been vitally important enough to warrant one since, it seemed, until now. Although, Latasha briefly pondered why a meeting had not been called when it was realised that the seers and the Knights could no longer bring forth life, for surely that was severe enough to warrant a gathering in order for a solution to be deciphered. Yet, that was long ago she sighed to herself as she shrugged the issue from her mind in order to concentrate on the current predicament at hand as her seer had decreed.

Despite the sparse number of seers and Knights that now remained, Calogero still appreciated things to be conducted with the correct amount of tradition and ceremony. This meant, all seers and Knights had been summoned to the 'great' hall. Not so great as the halls in past stories told thought Latasha bitterly. Especially since not even quite twenty sets of seers and Knights nearly filled it. There weren't many in that number that were younger than Calogero and Latasha but this did not mean that they commanded any less respect from their people.

"Seer Calogero Leventer and Knight Latasha Knower have summoned this meeting," announced Calogero in a bold voice filled with bass that carried strongly, "We have summoned you to discuss an impending and vitally important problem."

One Seer, who was slightly younger than the leading Seer and Knight pair cried out hopefully, "Have you discovered a solution to the breeding problem Calogero...can our kind have children again?"

Latasha grimaced in sudden surprise. Although the issue often danced through her mind, as it was never spoken of aloud, she had mistakenly thought that others had accepted their fate and given up hope of ever having the opportunity to see children smiling and laughing again amongst them. The realisation closed her throat, her chest became tight and she gulped in an attempt to suppress rogue tears that threatened to spill out over her eyes. Latasha did not want to see her kind to die out.

As a happy, excited muttering broke out amongst those gathered before them, Latasha clapped her hands together creating a booming clap of thunder with the help of a little Knight's magic in order to silence the crowd and to gain their attention again.

"Unfortunately, that grievous problem is something that we are still working on," uttered Latasha regretfully as she composed herself, "but Calogero requires your undivided attention now for something even more important still. Please listen to him carefully my friends."

Calogero patiently waited for complete silence to descend in the hall before he began speaking again.

"I understand your concern regarding that heart-breaking obstacle," his voice boomed out, "yet I require your aid despite it. I have received many visions over the past few months. They are concernedly very unclear to me and the only things that I can grasp from them are that they are vitally important and that they are paired with the phrase 'The Unfortunate's will be the doom of this world'. My Knight, Latasha and I have had no success in deciphering the real meaning or solution to them and so I need to know if any of you have had similar visions with anything along the same lines in them. I am of the thinking that if we can pool our knowledge together, we may be able to make something more of it. We are stronger together than standing alone, something we all know every day when we are see the blessing of our twinned Seer or Knight".

A small, lithe tigress stepped forward. Unlike Calogero she was slight and coyly nervous when speaking. Yet, she would not deny her leader when he called his people forward.

"Calogero" she began hesitantly, "I do not know if this is what you mean and truly, I do not want to waste your valuable time if it is not...but you did ask...and..."

"Do not be nervous my friend," Latasha softly said before Calogero could butt in with his brash need for succinct accounts, "anything at all that you have to offer us is useful, and as you rightly pointed out, we did indeed ask for your input"

Calogero had to admit begrudgingly to himself, that his Knight was far more adept at handling niceties than he was, and she had a knack for leading people in the right direction with a gentle hand.

The young tigress smiled weakly and cleared her throat with a little more confidence.

"Well, I would say, for months as well, that I have been seeing some kind of deformed creatures within my visions. Actually, in all honesty, at first it was just a sense of something that may be.

Then I felt certain that the creature was real. It is fanged, clawed, two-legged and really strong and fast. It started with just one of them but lately...every dream I have of them, there seems to be more and more, gorging on blood and wreaking destruction and havoc wherever they go, although I have heard no words or phrases such as you have done. I know I am often prone to flights of fancy, and my visions often have turned out to relate to things not worth noticing so I didn't want to bother anyone with it..."

Latasha's heart sank into the pit of her stomach and glancing to her companion, she could tell by his expression that his had done the same thing. If this was true, how could they have missed such an immense problem? Not for the first time, she wondered if Calogero's father's decision to leave the human world completely behind was a wise one. They were so isolated here and without interaction with other kinds they had even become withdrawn and unsociable amongst themselves.

An elderly Knight stepped forward too. His silver hair was long and braided in much the same fashion as Latasha's, bound with a plain leather thong. His vein-ridden hand rested on the Knight's sword still hung proudly at his bony hip, despite the fact that its use had not been required for numerous years now.

"Ahh, Sandro," breathed Calogero. He had much respect for the old warrior who was brash and old fashioned, much like himself.

"My old chum here has mentioned something quite similar to

those visions that have been mentioned sir," he announced sturdily. "Haven't you old friend," nodded Sandro, glancing over his shoulder encouragingly at his companion, an elderly tiger whose fur underneath his chin was peppered with silver streaks.

"Indeed, I have Calogero. Although I have not seen them wreaking havoc as just mentioned. Nevertheless, I have seen creatures that look much as just described, being 'born' if that is the right term of phrase. There were also Decona in my visions, although they did not feel as if the imposed any danger. In fact, they themselves were bleeding and their blood was what created the first of this new menace. It seems he was 'wrong' to start with and the blood could not contend with him. An uncovered, demonic malice lurking in his silent soul seized the magic of the Decona to turn it into something dangerous and dark that could be utilised against the world."

Calogero breathed a shallow sigh, not loud enough to be heard and disquiet the others, but enough for Latasha to see how worried he truly was.

"It seems that we have much to discuss my people."

21

Everhart and Loki had planned to leave on their journey right away, eager as they were to find others of their kind and Everhart's long missed parents, but it just did not seem honourable to leave the aged Mopsus alone and as they could not seem to encourage him to journey with them, they had ended up spending many more months with him than they had originally intended. Everhart had to admit that the time was indeed well spent and not only that, it was enjoyable. Apart from Loki, Everhart had not made many friends growing up, being the abandoned orphan kid didn't automatically propel you to most popular kid in a small group of insensitive youths. Not only did they learn much of the history of the seer's and the Knights that they should have by right grown up with during their time with the ancient feline, but Everhart had also been able to work on his patchy elemental talents and Mopsus had assured him in a voice steeped in pride that he was now somewhat of an expert in the manipulation of them. The three had become fast friends somewhere along the way, sharing stories, jokes and good company along with their meals, so it was heart wrenchingly sad when Mopsus passed away ending the merry trio's enjoyable time together. If it had not been for his unavoidable death, Loki wondered if he and Everhart would have ever found the heart or will to leave Mopsus to resume their adventure into the unknown. He could have willingly spent every day in the peaceful happiness that had materialised with the two seers.

Everhart and Loki had awoken one fine weathered morning to discover that the aged tiger was simply not present in the cool cave with them. Not a worrying occurrence in itself, but it was quite unusual for Mopsus to venture off for the day unaccompanied now, as the three of them had developed a bit of a routine in their time together as friends. They seemed to awaken naturally together every dawn, breakfast together every morning seated on the luscious green grass outside the opening of the cave and then spend the day together, every day, without fail, so the two companions consequently immediately felt that something was amiss. They had exited the cave without hesitation or the need for words, calling for Mopsus in turn and they had eventually found him stretched out by the cool, meandering river. Mercifully, he looked at peace with his huge eyes closed as if he was in a deep slumber, and Loki had uttered consolingly, that he had thought that Mopsus must have known that his time was ebbing close to its end and simply walked to the river to be at a place that brought him peace, lain down, gone to sleep and not woken back up. Everhart, having come to know and love the immense old cat, also had a suspicion that Mopsus would not have wanted them to wake up next to his deceased body in the fear of causing them distress. The tiger was as selfless as they came and would always think of others no matter what was happening to him. Many heartbroken tears were shed unashamedly. The loss was unbearable, especially being as it was so close in proximity to the loss of their heroine and friend Vita, and Everhart gravely dug a resting place next to Vita's in which to bury their good friend in. They spent several more days at the site that they had almost come to think of as home, not wanting to leave two close friends behind, alone, with no-one to sit beside them, but eventually Loki had encouragingly told Everhart that he thought both Mopsus and Vita would have wanted them to continue on, to find a safer place, and hopefully the rest of their kind, and so they had once again found themselves setting out travelling after solemnly promising that they would return in the future to visit two friends that had given them so much.

Before he had passed, Mopsus had provided them with much insight into where the seers and the Knights had intended to go, way back when he had travelled with them and so they therefore had a rough idea of which direction in which to head. Everhart lovingly placed a strong, companionable hand on Loki's broad, striped back as they walked along and it took the pair of them back to when it had just been the two of them in the beautiful and welcoming forest of Aither, before their days together had been seized by such shocking and dramatic events.

"We haven't talked together, just us two, in what feels like ages," commented Loki thoughtfully as they strolled along side by side at a relaxed pace, the long blades of green grass bending at their feet and the dramatic scenes that led them to this point falling to the back of their minds just as easily for the moment.

Everhart nodded easily and grunted deeply in agreement around a mouthful of juicy, green, apple, the cloudy juice of which dripped down the corner of his curved lip to settle in his uneven beard. Mopsus had been right about his eating habits changing, he had quickly gone off meat the more he had learned to control his flourishing elemental powers, the very smell of it cooking now made his stomach heave and he had to gulp down the urge to gag, but luckily Mopsus had taught him all the best places to forage for a satisfying vegetarian feast. He swallowed the refreshing fruit, core and all, down with an audible gulp and was finally able to form a more coherent response to Loki's observation.

"You're not wrong there my old friend. I think that we've been so busy running, learning and drowning in sorrow that we just haven't had the time to appreciate the small things."

Loki nodded with a wry smile upon his soft face. "Indeed, that is true enough. Yet now that we are alone again, I've remembered that I'd been meaning to mention something to both you and Mopsus for a couple of month's now. It just always seemed that it could wait, and I didn't want to obliterate the merry peace that we had established for ourselves"

Everhart was silent, allowing Loki to speak without interruption and distraction, but he did dip his head slightly to let his friend know that he was listening attentively and to carry on.

"I've been having some...disturbing visions of late, dark visions. I think that we may have a new problem to contend with along with the other miniscule one of saving our whole species from extinction, you know."

Everhart furrowed his dark eyebrows and brow in concern, and waved his glistening apple core in a half circular motion. "Go on," he bid his friend.

"Well, if my visions are to be believed and deciphered in the manner that I am inclined to think, there seems to be a new, disturbing, breed on the rise. One with a rather voracious appetite."

Everhart raised an eyebrow, as if to ask how this was their concern and to query its connection to them.

"I just know that it is important Everhart, although why this is so, I am unsure. I suggest that we keep it in mind."

Everhart never dis-regarded Loki's opinion, especially if it was the result of one of his visions.

"Ok, my friend. We'll do just that. Now, let's find somewhere to bed down for the night. It'll be dark in a bit and all this talk of nasty critters doesn't really put me in the mind for travelling in the moonlight alone."

*****

The fire had dwindled down to a few determined, glowing, embers but still was beautifully warm in the dark, night air. Everhart wasn't quite fully asleep and he could see Loki's long striped body curled belly first towards the heat through his half lidded eyes. The tiger's shadow flickered from side to side in an eerie dance with the fire's glow. Everhart stopped breathing as he studied it, his sleepiness evaporating instantaneously. There was another shadow within inches of Loki's, one that didn't belong to the great cat or anything else within their makeshift campsite.

Everhart sprang up fluidly, now graceful from months of practice with the guidance of Mopsus, and illuminated the darkness with a spark of crackling lightning. A hideous face glowered at him from the darkness, papery grey skin which contained eyes akin to pits of despair and glowing white fangs. The campsite erupted into a melee. The lighting had awoken Loki who dove for the creature instantaneously. Although, Loki had removed his fierce Decona weapon to sleep, his claws and fangs were still something to be feared. The intruder, having been spooked by the lightning hadn't yet moved and Loki's full weight slammed into him without mercy. The events of the past few months had taught the tiger not to delay and so, snarling he tore into his prey's shoulder savagely and without hesitation. Everhart's momentarily feeling of relief was shattered when unbelievingly the intruder flung his attacker from him like a rag doll. Loki's body bounced painfully on the ground as the creature turned, grinning wildly, towards Everhart. Its head now hung at a freakishly unnatural angle due to the missing chunks of shoulder and neck, but this horrific injury didn't seem to be bothering it much. Everhart fleetingly wondered why there was no blood gushing from the creature's wounds before the creature suddenly seemed to have closed the gap between them and with immense strength was attempting to wrestle Everhart and tilt his head back to expose his neck. The Knight instinctively knew that he couldn't win this battle of brute force, despite his own strength and power if he persisted. He was going to lose. Attempting to wriggle away to gain better purchase did no good and Everhart couldn't quite reach for his sword that lay on the ground where he had been sleeping. The fear that this may be the end of him and his friend after they had been through so much ignited Everhart's anger. He gripped the back of the creature's head; holding on to its greasy, black hair and ignited it in a ball of devastating fire.

 The creature screeched and let out an ear-splitting howl. The fire ate through him quickly as he flailed about, stumbling through the campfire. The flickers of flame from the campfire didn't even seem to touch the creature, yet the fire Everhart had produced just seemed to burn brighter and brighter. Everhart walked backwards around the site, edging towards Loki who still lay upon the ground but not willing to take his eyes from the creature. He knelt down, still eyeballing the living torch and laid a hand upon Loki's back. The great cat let out a mournful whimper.

"Can you get up Loki?" whispered Everhart. In answer, Loki heaved himself onto his four legs, wincing at the pain coursing along his back. He had landed awkwardly and would need to take it easy for a few days.

"Where's the monster?" Loki asked, crinkling his eyes at the pain in his back.

Glancing back to where the creature had been flailing around, Everhart was astonished to see that all that now remained was an ankle high pile of greasy, black ash. Smoke wisped from the top of the pile in lazy yet fanciful curves.

Everhart advance cautiously to the remains, dragging his sword with him. Unsheathing the blade, he nervously used it to poke the ash. The pile crumbled and a sudden breeze swished past to snatch handfuls of it and whisk it off into the night.

"I think that's him," he finally answered. "Damn glad Mopsus taught me to use that properly."

22

The Original Unfortunate, perched like a crow upon a high up grey, mossy, rock, surveyed his growing army with evident glee. It had only taken a few weeks to make this many Unfortunates and he almost gasped with delight at the thought of how many more he could make as time went on. Through trial and error it had become apparent that he was the only one of the Unfortunates that could bring another being like himself into existence. After making his first partner on the outskirts of Aither, they had tried time and time again under the order of the Original, unsuccessfully, for the new addition to make another creature himself. Yet, even following the process exactly as The Original had, each human that they caught and attempted to mutate simply perished after being bitten, no matter the quantity of blood that was drained from them. Their human hearts would just give out and they would drift off into oblivion. No other additions had been able to undertake the feat either, and so The Original had decided that he was an extraordinary and unique representation of his species, perhaps due to the fact that he was the first of his kind.

The other Unfortunates all obsequiously obeyed The Original unquestioningly and he had almost come to care for them in a strange fashion. He granted them permission to go out and prey on human victims alone at night, as long as they realised that their primary goal during these hunts was to return with detailed information as to where they had been, what the vicinity had looked like and how much food was there. The Original realised that keeping the Unfortunates fed was a daunting and imperative task if he was to achieve the glory and power that he imagined for himself. After creating just one more addition, to bring their total number to three, including The Original, they had decimated the village of Aither in less than an hour. Men, women and children all perished with no distinction. The sheer amount of dark blood that had been spilled had driven the two additional Unfortunates in to a vicious blood frenzy, and they had run riot unchecked, tearing the humans in their path limb from limb with ease. The Original had only managed to keep one Aither resident alive to be transformed into an Unfortunate. That episode was the reason he had decreed that The Unfortunates were to hunt alone, if he allowed them to decimate humanity in that fashion continuously, as and when they desired, their food source would soon reach a critical low. His creatures were invincible anyway, so it seemed, so there was no danger to them in hunting solo.

The Original gazed out amongst the forest that they had now adopted as their temporary home. It had been the perfect spot. The towering trees were so plentiful and grew so close together that virtually no sunlight made it through the thick canopy of branches to reach the forest floor, causing it to smell rancid and dank. Once they had set up there, all other life had scattered in haste and so all that could be heard was the low murmuring of Unfortunate voices. No bird calls or grasshopper chirrups spoilt the atmosphere. It was now a place suitable for The Unfortunates only, where their raven black hair and eyes were the same as everyone else in their species. The Original was the only one who, once transformed, had retained his original hair colour from his previous existence. He still possessed his long, waist-length, bone-white hair. Only now, instead of being dank and matted, the hair shone gloriously to match his curved, perfectly white teeth. His eyes, however, were the same as the rest of his novel creations, but as he could not remember whether his eyes were this way before or not, it did not bother him at all.

A low hubbub erupted from his people below. That night's hunters must have returned and would soon be with him with a report on what they had seen and where they had ventured that night. There were twenty-five of them in existence now, so the Original had decided to allow five a night to go out hunting individually at the moment. The others were a bit discontent at having to wait that long for food and moreover for the rich tang of metallic blood to fill their mouths, as their hunger was ferocious at this point, but they did not truly seem to need to consume anything in order to remain alive. Their strength and speed never diminished, regardless of how little or how infrequently they ate.

The need to eat was more of a mental need and urge but it drove them on all the same. Obedient as they were, the returned Unfortunate's came to him immediately to report as was required of them. Four grey-coloured faces stood before him.

"There are only four of you before me," commented The Original, "where is the fifth hunter?"

The four shook their heads regretfully.

"We have not seen him since we split up to hunt my Lord!" One uttered in response. "Nor heard him in the night. He has vanished to our senses."

The Original posed more questions to his subjects in order to gain further information as to what had become of the fifth hunter, but no-one had any ideas as to where the other Unfortunate might be. They presented their reports on how successful they had been on their hunting trips and by the end of their summaries the fifth Unfortunate still had not returned to the forest to report. The Original dismissed them and pondered where he could have gone. He was doubtful that the Unfortunate could have abandoned the pack. Their fealty was unwavering and unforced, the Original had never had to demand anything from them or utilise threats to have them carry out his wishes. Yet what other explanation could there be? The Original decided he would have to enforce hunting from now on in packs of two, with strict orders not to decimate everything in sight, just to be sure of what was going on.

23

Some of the Decona people were silently angry with her decision, some were seething. They would never contemplate contradicting her decisions directly, or disobeying her orders but their anger seethed quietly amongst them. Shesha sighed heavily to herself. This was the first time in an extremely long time that any of her people had died in such a horrific and intrusive manner. It was simple brutal murder. In truth, deaths of any kind were infrequent among the Decona as they remained elusive from the ever-growing human population and they were in no danger from any natural predator due to their size, strength, skills and intelligence. This was the very reason that her people were so utterly incensed. It was thought by many, that it was far too coincidental that the very time that they dropped their guard enough to let a human enter their world, one of their own had been savagely taken from them. The Decona felt as if they had been taken advantage of and felt foolish for it, and feelings of foolishness often evolved into feelings of anger. Added to the ominous warnings that the seer had left them with, many of the Decona had wanted to hunt down the human that had been in their home for answers, under the impression that he had led someone to them, and some even wanted to hunt the seer too! Shesha had strictly forbidden that course of action under any circumstances and reminded her kin that it was not just any human that they were baying for, but a Knight of the ancient line that they talked about. She had no idea what had happened to the young Decona child at the entrance to their home, but she adamantly refused to contemplate that it could have been the fault of their two visitors. She was not such a bad judge of character.

No-one had discovered the stiffening body of the boy before he had already bled out onto the cold, unforgiving ground. Shesha regretted this desperately, not only because his memories and knowledge had been forever lost to them, meaning that they would never know what had happened to him, but also because the child had perished utterly alone, with no comfort from a friendly face. A lone, salty tear dripped from the polished scales of Shesha's cheek and meandered its way down her face to track down to her slender chin. She smeared it away in irritation with a perfectly clawed finger. What use was there in crying about the tragedy now she thought angrily to herself! She had a duty and an obligation to protect her people and she needed to give them some sense of stability. Shesha understood that some of the people were right in part of their requests. A tracking party should be sent to track down the seer and his Knight she considered. Not to hack them mercilessly to death as she knew that some angry Decona hoped for, but instead, to find out more of the threat that they had been warned of and whether this death was the start of it and to learn what the great seer knew. Loki's words that he had left them with were now more poignant than ever and she would not let her people face the new world completely in the dark and alone whilst there was something she could do about it.

Shesha picked up a delicately crafted silver bell from her desk between webbed thumb and forefinger to ring it. The bell was always kept upon her sturdy, polished oaken desk and was embedded with rich, dark green stones that served as decorations for the etched eyes of bowing Decona. The eyes twinkled sweetly and gleefully as the bell's chime rang out into the evening's silence.

A short, stocky Decona appeared without delay in her doorway, wrapped in a gracious, golden, silk robe from scaled head to clawed toe.

"Yesss, Lady Shesha," he sang sweetly, bowing slightly and stretching out his arm with his hand curved towards himself to steady his balance.

"Organise a search party without delay," she commanded without explanation. "I will be leading them myself. Don't tarry Mei. We shall be leaving at twilight. I require just two companions to be selected for this journey. I trust in you to make the appropriate choices of companions without my intervention."

Mei dutifully dipped his rounded head in deference and turned to organise Shesha's bidding without comment.

"And Mei," Shesha called firmly behind him, "let it be known that this is not a hunting party. The Decona seek the seer and his Knight in these troubled times for aid only. I shall leave you to keep order in my stead whilst I am away and I expect you to ensure thoroughly that my decree is known and respected by all our people"

Mei turned back towards Shesha and gracefully crossed the cool, stone floor to meet her. Dropping all usual protocol, he took her slender right hand between his soft palms firmly yet gently. Squeezing her scaled hand, he flashed a tender, toothy smile at her that instantly brightened his usually reserved features.

"Shesha, you are not only my leader, but also my friend. I trust fully in you and your decisions, for I know that they are always made selflessly and with what is best for our people in mind. Trust in me too dear one. Any decision that I am required to make in your absence will be as if you had made it yourself. And as I said, I do this not only because you have asked me to as our leader, but also because I am your friend and would ensure that the right decisions are made for the right reasons whether you asked it of me or no."

Mei did not wait for a response from the figurehead of their people, but turned steadily on his heels and headed out of the doorway, his golden robe billowing out in the breeze behind him. Shesha felt blessed to know such a person and to count him as a friend.

24

Loki's broad back and hips had been severely painful for several days after the alarming attack, so the pair had taken their travelling as easy as possible up until now. They had travelled slowly and almost leisurely, by daylight hours only, and ensured that they looked for a secure, defensive place to camp each night, hours in advance of when they actually needed to bed down. Deep caves and the uppermost reachable tree branches served as sleeping places now, the pair thinking that these may be a bit safer and more difficult to stumble across, if a bit less comfortable than previous campsites and also give them a bit more time if something happened to attack them again. They did not wander to squander any opportunity that they had to gain an advantage against attackers in the night. Luckily they had not had the misfortune of coming into contact with any more of those monstrous creatures since the last encounter. Now that Loki was feeling brighter the two had picked up their pace and had seemed to leave the comfortable fertile lands behind them. Whilst everything was still green and growing here, the heat had become unbearably oppressive and they were constantly plagued by swarms of buzzing biters. Irritating trickles of sweat dripped from Everhart's lined brow from the constant and unrelenting humidity. He was tempted to whip up a bit of a breeze for some relief from the oven like temperature with his new found skills, yet Loki frowned upon using the magic at any given moment, possessing wariness that it would attract un-needed attention.

Walking along in companionable silence, Everhart and Loki both picked up the splashing noise immediately, Loki's rounded ears curving instinctively towards the sound. Everhart placed a single finger to his lips and quietly motioned for Loki to remain standing still. It was still a bright day and the sun glared at them from the clear sky so Everhart had doubted that one of those creatures would attack under these circumstances but he could be mistaken. Suddenly, a dripping wet tiger came bounding through the foliage followed by a giggling young woman. They halted unceremoniously as soon as their eyes met Loki and Everhart's, seemingly just as surprised as Loki and Everhart were to meet two strangers in the middle of nowhere. Strangely, the tiger began to growl aggressively and its fur bristled angrily upon its back and shoulders. Its black lips curled back intimidatingly, revealing an impressive row of sharp white teeth as it snarled menacingly. The woman behind it looked nearly as angry too, and Everhart half fancied that if she curled her lips back he would see a matching set of grinding teeth.

"Why are you here!" she yelled shrilly, "We've kept out of your way and caused no trouble, now leave us be!"

Loki's confused expression was a mirror reflection of the image that adorned Everhart's face.

"Please do not be afraid, for we intend you no harm," Loki ventured calmly, but before he could continue the woman interrupted angrily.

"Afraid!" she shrieked hysterically, "Afraid!!"

She flapped her damp arms wildly, screeching and babbling incoherently. Flecks of spittle sprayed on to her chin as she shrieked, making her erratic behaviour all the more bewildering. Everhart decided that she was quite mad, and as he looked more closely at her, he noticed that her right eye only was a bright, emerald green, just like Loki's and his. The left eye, however, was clouded over and appeared dead in her face, almost as if she had been afflicted with terrible cataracts, although Everhart thought that she looked far too young for that particular affliction, about his age if he was not mistaken. He was so lost in studying the woman and the absurd scene of her antics, that if it was not for Loki's bellowing warning call, he would have been caught completely unawares.

"Ever! The tiger!" roared in a panic-filled tone.

The dripping tiger was already in mid-launch towards himself. Everhart didn't know entirely what was going on, but he was almost certain that the pair had been a seer and a Knight, and he did not want to cause them any harm if he could help it. Instead, Everhart instinctively summoned thick bands of air as fast as he could and wrapped the oncoming attacker up in them, a handy trick that Mopsus had taught him whilst he was alive.

"It's not always all about aggressive attack young man," he had admonished him one afternoon, "sometimes you need to keep your head and your wits about you and consider that defence really might be the best option at certain times. What if, for instance, you do not want to injure your attacker and you require them in full health?"

With that the old tiger had leapt playfully upon him and proceeded to attempt to lick him to death with a rough tongue. When Everhart had burst out laughing, Mopsus had sternly told him to defend himself against the 'attack' without causing harm to himself. It had taken Everhart days and days to figure out a solution, until the elderly tiger had reminded him that he had use of ALL of the elements that nature provided, and to cease to be so obsessed with always utilising lightning.

Seeing the wet tiger suspended uncomfortably in the air, the crazed woman shrieked wildly and then began to run at Everhart with no care for herself. He braced himself to dodge and catch the woman, his plan to twist and tumble her to the ground, but before she reached him, older human voices yelled out.

"Please do not hurt them!"

The distressed voices were just enough to distract Everhart so that the female ploughed with an audible thud into him, roughly knocking him to the grassy ground. As her hands reached eagerly around his unprotected throat, he suddenly matched the new voices to the faces that were still kept in his mind.

There stood his parents.

25

His mother's lengthy hair still wisped artfully around her face, just as he remembered it had when he was just an care-free, curious lad, but where it had once been a rich, glorious chestnut brown hue, it now held more silver-grey than anything else. The wrinkles that were now etched in her heart shaped face had never been there before either and the same went for the strained, worrisome expression that was now written upon her aged face. The ragged, faded, azure blue shawl pulled closely around her slight, stooped shoulders was also a stark testament to the changes that had ravaged her over the missing years. When Everhart was a small lad, she was most particular about everything being neat, clean and tidy and every single aspect of her had gleamed with health and radiant perfection.

His father looked as equally tired and hard done by. The joyous, laughing man that he had looked up to so fervently was now replaced by a squat, serious looking being. His tidy, dark brown hair was now unkempt and patchy, mostly grey like his mothers. His eyes were watchful and wary, and a hairy, pale arm had stretched out protectively in front of his wife although it quivered with fear. His cold eyes glared at him untrusting and Everhart realised that the man did not recognise him for who he was.

Loki had silently padded over to him whilst all this commotion had been unfolding and the great tiger now gently and carefully picked up the woman from atop of him, who was doing her best to strangle Everhart to death, by the collar on her tattered shirt. Surprisingly the woman went limp in his grasp, like a cub being moved about by the tender touch of its mother. He gracefully deposited the woman on the ground and spoke to her sternly,

"Now my dear, if you could be so gracious as to just sit there quietly and cease all this nonsense, I can see about getting your friend released post haste."

Oddly, the woman looked abashed and embarrassed, like a small child caught stealing cooling pies from a windowsill, and folded her arms in front of her and jutted her bottom lip out petulantly whilst dipping her head down to stare at her empty lap.

At this point, still with features laden with wariness, Everhart's parents rushed over to the woman, crouching down beside her and enveloping her in their arms. Everhart felt an unexpected lump stick in his throat as his eyes stung with unshed tears. Loki knew his friend too well and could see what was going on but he took control of the situation by nudging Everhart subtly, who was still sat upon the ground, with a friendly, cold, wet nose and gesturing over to the other tiger, still floating a metre or so above the ground, encased safely in a prison of sheer air.

He spoke gently, but loud enough for his voice to carry, "Everhart. Do you think you could let the tigress there down now?

I think that we have the situation under control."

"Everhart?! Not Everhart Egidius Bovenwater?" blurted the Knight's mother and father simultaneously, jaws dropping and mouths left gaping wide open. Their eyes darted back and forth between each other and the duo.

Before replying, Everhart undid the sturdy knots of air holding the tigress in place and carefully lowered her to the ground before releasing her entirely. The tigress, still snarling angrily, stalked not towards Everhart, but to the sulking woman and his parents hunched together on the ground. They looked like a family, and Everhart felt like an intruder. Loki nudged himself under Everhart's arm reminding him that he was still here, and gently encouraged him up. Despite realising he sounded like a sorrowful child, Everhart started with

"Why did you not come back for me?" his voice broke slightly and he cleared his throat in an attempt to disguise it, "I had feared you were both long dead."

Answering tears welled up in the eyes of both his mother and his father, they rose to their bare, scuffed feet, but Everhart noticed that they still did not take their hands from the woman or move from her and the tigress forward towards him. His father spoke first, and his words begrudgingly lifted Everhart's spirits despite wanting to remain angry at their abandonment of him.

"Oh my little Knight, you turned out just as strong and perfect as   I   knew   you   always   would."

26

Loki and Everhart spent days and days talking with his parents, the woman and the tigress and they soon uncovered many facts that rearranged their perspective on their lives up to the present day. It seemed that the woman and the tigress were indeed connected to the seers and the Knights, more deeply than they had imagined, but not in the way that they had expected. Everhart's parents told him of how they had arrived at the habitation of the seers and the Knights many years ago, and of how they had spoken with their leader. They described him as a brash, unsympathetic figure, despite having an adolescent son already, who had informed them disparagingly, that simply having green eyes meant nothing at all, and that their kind were not welcome to remain with them. They had been permitted to stay for just a few days before the leader had heavily suggested that they may wish to leave and head back to where they belonged. Nevertheless, his mother had informed him after much hugging and tears, these few days were more than ample time for dark rumours to reach their ears. Not all the seers and Knights were unwelcoming she advised. From others, there were hushed murmurs and whispers of how the leader's mate had had two twin cubs, one male and one female, a number of years back. Meant to be a delight for the seers, the event had not been quite as joyous as it should have been. Apparently, one of the cubs, the female, had been born 'wrong' as had the Knight that had been born to match it. The other cub, although he had not had any birth defects, did not have a Knight to match it at all, there being so few humans with the pack since they had uprooted and moved, and the leader was angry and embarrassed at what his line had produced. It seemed that the tigress cub was nothing but what she appeared to be. An ordinary tigress, not capable of visions as any seer should be and not fit to be called a seer at all. The Knight was equally as unfit for her duty, born with only one emerald green Knight's eye with the other clouded over like that of a dead fish. The pair had been instantly segregated from the rest of the pack on the orders of the leader and they had remained so for many years. However, even though they were still children, as they grew, the leader realised that in time, he may have a problem with them as they got older. He did not want either of them breeding and 'infecting' and diluting their species, and so he ordered for them to be 'put to sleep' by suffocation. The mother of the tigress could not bear it and so, fearing also for the life of her son who the leader stolidly ignored, stole both cubs away along with the addled child Knight. This episode occurred only a few days prior to his parents arriving with the seers and the Knights and feeling that it was their duty to aid those that were more vulnerable than themselves, they had left in search of the refugees. Needless to say, they did discover them, and they had helped them as best as they were able to. Everhart's parents had eventually divulged their reasons for travelling this far to the mother and the three parents had excitedly decided, that perhaps the green-eyed boy, left behind in Aither, could be the missing Knight destined to have been born for her seer son. The three of them had come to a pact that the humans would stay here, in the wilderness, and protect the young girls, whilst the cub's mother took her son to accompany her to retrieve Everhart from the far away village of Aither and bring him back to them.

That was the last that they had ever seen or heard of the pair and Everhart's parents had sorrowfully believed that it had meant that the worst imaginable fate had happened and their son and the two tigers were no more. They had decided to stay in the wilderness and raise the two children that they still had in their care instead, despite being ill equipped to do it. They were careful to avoid any areas that the rest of the pack were likely to tread, doubting that they would receive any mercy if the seer leader had been prepared to put mere children to death, simply so that they did not breed.

At this point in the telling of the story, the woman had interjected with a mad cackle and beamingly announced, "And because they did not want us to breed, I said the words so that they could not breed either."

Everhart's mother had absent-mindedly patted the woman's

slight shoulder with a consoling, "Now now Athena, do not let this upset you again my petal. Set those dreams of score settling and revenge from your heart. You know that is not our way." Continuing on with the story, although in all honesty, there was not a great deal left to tell.

Loki had quickly put together that the tigress was a twin to him, although he was quite distressed that he could not remember her, or nothing prior to Everhart discovering him in the forests of Aither, not even what had become of his mother.

Loki's sister, Freya, had been coyly shy on the discovery of her sibling, yet the two tigers seemed genuinely happy to have re-discovered each other. Everhart's parents were equally overjoyed also, particularly so when they had heard that their son had not only spent many years with Loki as a friend, but that the pair of them had actually gone searching for them when they had discovered that they had actually gotten this far on their quest.

"Always said that my little Knight had his hear and his mind in the right place," his father had announced proudly and had promptly and boldly pulled the muscly Everhart into an emotional embrace. Everhart realised that he had been correct in his assumptions when they had first re-encountered the group days ago. The group were a family, but Loki and himself, it seemed, were included members also.

27

The Unfortunate horde continued to increase in number, although now their progress advanced more slowly than before, now that the Original was taking precautionary measures. He preferred to remain in the forest to supervise his people, rather than leave often to bring forth new Unfortunate creations to serve in his army. No more members of his coven, as he liked to think of it, had gone missing since the first, but neither had the missing member returned to him and none of the hunting packs had sighted him or any sign that he had been around the vicinity. Most odd he thought to himself, being as they were such loyal subjects and practically invincible in this pathetic world. Members of his horde now hunted in packs of three on his specific orders, and as ferocious as they were, despite his instructions to restrain themselves, they had nearly decimated most surrounding human life. The widespread murder of a species that he had once belonged to, did not concern him at all, but the fact that the ready food supply was waning did worry him somewhat. Picking his white fangs idly with a pale finger, he decided that it may be time to move on from this forest very soon, to grounds that had richer pickings. A nomadic life may better suit their purposes he mused and he had always imagined that their current living arrangements were at most, a temporary measure. The Original glided down to the ground smoothly and noiselessly from his usual haunt upon his mossy rock and called clearly for the burly Unfortunate that he had managed to recruit in Aither to attend him. The large being had fast become his valued right hand within his self-created army. He now utilised the previous Aither resident for most of the communication between himself and the rest of The Unfortunates, so that he did not have to issue his orders to them directly himself.

The Unfortunate had still managed to retain his bulk on being made into one of them and it gave the Original a great deal of amusement that such a hulk could move so quickly and so soundlessly. He even actually enjoyed the Unfortunate's company to a certain extent, although he certainly did not love the being. Love, he decided, was something that he and his kind were quite incapable of, although he did feel a kind of affinity towards him, akin to that he had felt towards somebody else in a previous place and time, somebody that he had followed once. He could not quite grasp the memory that eluded him in the darkness of his mind, each time he reached for it, it slid through his fingers of his mind like a slippery, blood spattered drained corpse and so he abandoned it, bringing his attention back to the present and the issues that needed his attention currently.

"Do you have orders Creator?" queried the bulky Original obsequiously with an ungainly bow.

"Yes. We need to move on to more plentiful hunting grounds

with due haste. Ensure that no-one is scheduled to hunt tonight and that they are ready to move. We leave tonight. I have a mind to increase my force and I am unable to do that with the lack of prey now in the vicinity."

The instructed bobbed his oversized head obediently and hastily vanished to spread his master's word as quickly as possible. The Original smiled in gleeful anticipation. More humans to hunt meant that there would be many more opportunities for new Unfortunates to be created as he desired. His army would continue to expand and he would be a force to be reckoned with in this world. No one would deign to order him around and treat him with contempt. Any who did would rue the day that they had been born into this God forsaken world.

28

The flickering flames of the fire danced eerily in the deep darkness of the night. Since the monster attack on their travels, Everhart and Loki had instinctively taken charge of the new family situation and decided to ensure that their group kept a designated watch at all times of day and night, regardless of how tired anyone was. No good could come of any risk of being approached unawares, especially now that they had more people to care for who were starkly more vulnerable than themselves. They had to protect and defend them and it was time to stop just thinking of their own hides, Everhart had pointed out. Leadership appeared to come more easily to him now that he was not seeking it out intently. Loki had generously volunteered to take the first stint of keeping watch, as everyone else was greatly fatigued and so he was now sat alone by the fireside whilst his family slept soundly mere feet away from him - his family. The words sounded odd yet beautiful in his mind. He could not believe that he actually had a true sister of his own, although, no matter how hard he tried, he could not possibly comprehend how their father could have abandoned her so willingly, let alone sentenced her to a cruel death, simply because she was not blessed with visions like the rest of the seers. If the visions were the blessing they were made out to at all he mused thoughtfully. He had no control over the visions that were thrust upon him and so he was at their mercy at all times. He was reviled and saddened by his father's actions but resolved to learn a hard lesson from them. With the good-natured Mopsus being the only other seer that he had met previously, he had naively thought that his race were always honourable and just and above the petty spitefulness and greed of humans. Yet these recent discoveries were a lesson that any creature could make an incorrect decision, whether they were sent divine guidance or not. It was their choice alone as to whether they heeded the information that they were presented with. As the thought crossed his mind, one of his visions violently slammed into him with no prior warning. His mind and eyes were roughly seized with colours and vision and noise all at once, overwhelming all his other senses. The visions were not always a pleasant experience for the seer receiving them. He saw himself front on and where he was now, this very campsite, with his family asleep besides him in the positions that he had witnessed them last. Behind him in the darkness, were not just one as before, but three of the horrific creatures that had attacked them previously, advancing towards the resting group with murderous intent gleaming in their soulless eyes. Their curved teeth were gleaming in the darkness, eager to sink them into the throats of his loved ones.

The disturbing vision was thankfully brief, but he had received enough warning for action to be taken immediately. He recognised the setting and there was no doubt that the warning could have come sooner. The attack could happen at any moment and was likely to from what his senses told him. He would not allow this fortuitous guidance to go unheeded. He dashed to Everhart immediately and woke him first before waking the others as quickly as he could, to explain his vision hurriedly in fretful tones and darting glances. Everhart knew to take Loki seriously and was up and organising the party with haste, wasting not a minute as if he had not been asleep just a moment before. Loki stood protectively in front of the humans, the hairs on his shoulders, neck and back bristling with both fear and anger, his black lips curled back revealing curved, deadly white fangs that could easily match those of the oncoming creatures. His kind and playful nature had been placed aside in order to protect those around him. Freya stood alongside him looking just as formidable, her quivering lips pulled back to reveal an identical snarling set of jaws and teeth. Everhart stood slightly away from the party hoping to draw the attack to himself first and give the others more of a fighting chance, his hand touching his sword at his hip through force of habit. The last creature that they had fought had seemed most interested in him than anything else and he was hoping events would unfurl in the same manner this time. Athena smiled crookedly with a mischievous glint in her good eye and stepped away from the tigers to stand with Everhart.

"Get back with the others," whispered Everhart in a frustrated murmur, waving his free hand to gesture her softly away, "I won't be able to concentrate my fire at them if I'm trying to protect you at the same time and I don't want you to get hurt. Loki and Freya will protect you."

Athena was not deterred by his reluctance to accept her offered aid.

"I'll protect you instead brother," she promised.

Everhart was too overwhelmed and too worried to show his happiness at her naming of him in their current predicament. He was still concerned for her safely and would have preferred to draw the attack alone. He would willingly sacrifice himself for this group if that was what was required of him. However, before he could explain this to Athena and get her to stand with the others in order to be safer from the impending danger, the monsters appeared as Loki had warned that they would.

Just as Loki had foreseen, there were three of the beasts. Walking night terrors in their midst. Without waiting to see what they would do, Everhart seized the initiative, not wasting the element of surprise that they had been gifted with and unleashed a bolt of blazing fire at the centre of their group. It hit the middle creature square in its wide chest and shrieking, he was immediately engulfed within the crackling flames which licked hungrily up his torso, almost as quickly as the creatures themselves moved, and travelled speedily down his arms and legs. The other two creatures were too quick for Everhart to target straight after and they separated from the living torch in a blink of an eye. Everhart swung around in the darkness, his bright eyes searching for the creatures, whilst he remained breathlessly alert. A deep set of twin growls sounded to his right and drew his gaze. The remaining two monsters were about to descend on his family. Yet the beasts were not close together and Everhart knew he would struggle to defeat them both at the same time with his Knight's fire. Desperately he shot a plume of flame at one, knowing that the delay may mean death for someone in the party. At the same time, Athena sang out gracefully;

"I say you cannot reach them and so reach them you cannot!"

As Everhart's target screeched in agony and burnt into soft, grey, ash, his gaze shot to the remaining creature. It had attempted to continue to the gathered humans and tigers ignoring Athena's outburst, sensing now that they were in fact the easier target of the available prey, but he had seemed to bounce off some invisible shield that encompassed his family within it when he had reached out for them. The creature snarled and looked accusingly towards the two Knights, seeming to know where his new obstacle had originated from. Everhart held out his arm steadily, ready to aim another shot of his fire at the intruder, but the creature seemed to realise that it could no longer succeed and it flitted away faster than could be thought possible if one had not faced them before. Everhart let out a breath that he did not know he had been holding and sprinted to his family, who he was able to reach with no problem, no barrier remained to stand in his way and halt his steps. They were thankfully unharmed, if understandably panicked. Everhart swung his head around on his neck in Athena's direction. She stood there with a gleeful smile on her face and giggled happily, wringing her hands together and systematically popping each of her knuckles.

"Athena, that was you, wasn't it?!" he smiled astonished, already knowing the answer to his question.

Freya answered instead, in a proud, sisterly voice.

"You shouldn't write Athena's abilities off, brother Knight. Others have, to their detriment. She may not think in the same way as you or I do, but she is a Knight nonetheless, whatever others may say. And as you can see, she has some of the powers that you do, although no-one has ever taught us. I like to think that I was not born useless either and it was just that I was born to protect her instead of the other way around, because she is special."

Everhart smiled happily and nodded, "Well it looks like I'd be wise to remember that doesn't it." He turned back to Athena. "Good thinking Athena my friend. You're pretty good with that air trick. Do you know it took me ages to think of doing that and that was with somebody teaching me how it was done. Looks like you could teach me a few things as well."

Athena danced a bizarre jig on the spot, overjoyed with the obvious praise and letting it show with some high pitched giggling and hand clapping.

Freya beamed at him and nodded her head gratefully, acknowledging her gratitude at his praise of her closest friend. The rest of his family smiled gratefully also.

"What did I tell you," his father grinned joyfully, "that Knight of ours has his heart in the right place."

Everhart blushed and took a sudden interest in his feet whilst Loki, Freya and his mother joined Athena in her giggling.

29

"Fire?" queried the Original sceptically, raising a pale white eyebrow and tapping an elegant fingernail against his slender arm, "but you are as aware as I am that we are completely impervious to fire! I could stand in a campfire for hours and not have it so-much as smoulder my feet!"

The Original had thought that he was incapable of and above human emotions now that he had exited that species and been remade in his new, superior form. Actually, he was not sure whether he had even been capable of them before being remade either, but now he knew that he had been mistaken, for now he was furiously angry at the thought that one of his own would dare to lie to him!

"It was not any ordinary fire, Master," squirmed the Unfortunate on the ground in front of him uncomfortably, "the male human shot the fire right out of his outstretched fingers and it stuck to the others immediately. I swear it is the truth! They were burnt to nothing but grey ash within minutes. I would have been happy to take the human on Master, but I thought that you would rather learn of this weapon that they wield, than not know of it if I failed in my attack."

The Original Unfortunate clenched and unclenched his vein ridden, pale fist, digging his sharpened fingernails into the palm of his hand in an attempt to dissipate his growing anger. He controlled the quiver in his voice as best as he could in order to hide the rage that was building up inside his chest. He did not want petty human emotions to impede his extraction of all the relevant information from his creation cowering on the cool earth before him.

"Have you anything else useful to report to me?" he asked in a low, raspy voice.

The Unfortunate nodded quickly, not wanting to meet the furious gaze of his creator and instead staring intently at the ground he knelt on as he spoke.

"The one that had the magic fire was also possessed of the most unusual green eyes, brighter than any ordinary human being's eyes that I have ever seen. It may not have been significant on its own Master, but another one of the humans did had one eye the same colour as this male and she seemed to be able to use some sort of magic as well. She did not use the fire that the male did, but she conjured up some strange force field instead that seemed to be an obstacle between me and my prey. There were two big, striped cats with these unusual humans, although only one of these had the same unusual emerald green eyes and they were no match for our strength on their own. They were all in the company of two other humans but these did not seem to be of any significance and appeared as ordinary humans to my senses. It was the smell of all the human blood so close together that drove us to hunt the group initially."

The Original abruptly turned away from the Unfortunate and began to run the facts that he had just learned through his twisted, devious mind. He felt that he had all the information that he now required for plotting his next course of action and he needed no further information from his creation, so he ignored him entirely.

The burly, right hand of the Original Unfortunate, ever present now at The Original's side, heaved the informant up off the ground unceremoniously and with obvious ease.

"I suggest you disappear now, you are no longer needed here."

He released him from his iron-like grip after speaking the order and the informant vanished immediately, before he had even had a chance to hit the ground again.

The Original danced his long, black nails, across his slim, pale chin, ignoring this exchange between two not as important as himself. Some of the details of the story that he had just heard were unnervingly familiar to him, although he could not quite recall why this should be the case. There was something before this life that the information clicked within his distant memories. Someone that he had been with that had connections to these bright eyed creatures...that was it! The two of them had been chasing down beings with bright, emerald green eyes! As far as his broken memories served him, they had not possessed an ability to wield any sort of magic to his knowledge, but they were still a threat nonetheless and they had to be destroyed. That much the Original now remembered and vowed to re-kindle his previous mission of ridding the world of these oddities.

"I want those green-eyed beings tracked down as soon as possible," he ordered sternly. "Not killed however. Not at first anyway. I do not want them having a chance to use this death-fire on a small party of ours before we manage to learn anything, so do not allow them to be engaged until I order this course of action to be followed. Send a small pack of Unfortunates to track them down and instruct them to report their location back to me immediately once they have been discovered."

The burly Unfortunate nodded succinctly and hastened off to do his master's bidding with no questions asked and with no delay.

Twirling his lengthy, white hair around a long, painfully bony finger, the Original embraced the rush of anticipation coursing through his lithe body. He relished these new feelings along with the thought of taking on this new foe. Humans were no challenge to him and his kind and he relished the thought of witnessing the terror and the recognition of unworthiness in the green eyes of his prey, moments before their souls were ripped from their bodies. He cracked his knuckles systematically in a human manner and popping noises issued from his fingers as he smirked from his longing for death. He vowed his wishes would not go long without being fulfilled.

30

Latasha nervously thrummed her slender fingers against her curved knee as she gazed upon Calogero's black and amber striped body as it twitched and jerked violently and intently at her tapping feet. The large tiger's emerald green eyes were unnervingly wide open through the twitching and shot through with stark blood-red veins that snaked eagerly across the whites of his eyeballs, although he was unresponsive in any other way. He had been in this unnerving state for at least half an hour now, longer than any vision that had seized his mind and body previously, yet Latasha knew better than to attempt to rouse him from the vision's unbreakable grasp. She could see that he was still breathing so at least that was something. More often than not, his visions would only visit him momentarily whilst he was awake and were so swift that if he had not mentioned them, Latasha would have been unaware that anything had happened at all sometimes. Nevertheless, there were these rare occasions when the visions would seize his body and mind completely and mercilessly, although not usually for this worrisome length of time. If it was not for Latasha's protective presence at the seer's side, at times like this he would be completely defenceless and vulnerable to any nearby malice waiting to visit mischief upon him. At times like this, a Knight's duty was thrust upon her and her purpose in being a protector was starkly evident. Suddenly, the great tiger stopped moving completely so that not even his chest was falling and rising.

An agonising roar ripped from Calogero's throat without warning as he came back to reality suddenly.

"Calogero?" she queried hesitantly, the name in itself a question. This pained vocal reaction from him was also something new to her in a situation such as this. Calogero rarely deviated from his usual unshakable, reserved demeanour, and he was certainly never known to cry out at any time, especially when a vision had visited him. She cautiously placed her hand on her companion's well-muscled shoulder.

The tiger's wild gaze shot to her warily and she became frightened at the own fear that she could see in her counterpart's whiskered face, who at this moment looked like any wild-eyed and frightened ordinary animal. If Calogero was frightened, that meant that there was something chilling indeed to be frightened of. The seer was not prone to flights of nervousness and he was not scared of anything at all that she could think of. He was always one to meet any opponent, obstacle or challenge head on without shrinking from it, regardless of any danger to himself.

The uncharacteristic fear did not dissipate even when Calogero finally recognised the face of his loyal Knight and he simply barked out, "We need to find my brother and sister, we need to find them now, before the world is torn asunder by teeth and claws of the night!". He flipped himself over, landing deftly on his feet and shook out his body as if trying to rid himself of some parasite.

"Brother and sister?" she mouthed back, silently and almost dumbly with an incredulous raised eyebrow. "You surely don't mean the twins Calogero? My friend, you are well aware that neither hide nor hair of them has been seen since your mother stole them away as cubs. Are you even sure that they are still alive? It is highly doubtful that they and your mother would have made it alone in the wilderness, and even if they were alive, why do they need to be found now? Your father was adamant that they were a curse upon our people and assured us all that they needed to be removed."

The fear in Calogero's face shrank back, not disappearing entirely, but making enough room for some anger and disappointment too. His eyes became less wide and narrowed slightly as he addressed Latasha.

"That is the first time that you have ever questioned one of my visions Latasha. I sincerely hope that it is the last. And you are well aware that my father wanted Freya killed, not simply removed, you are just too uncomfortable to confirm it aloud. I would not say this to anyone else living, but my father was at best, an overly-proud fool who did not give his visions the true credit that they deserved as any true seer should. In case you are otherwise mistaken, I am not my Father and never have been nor will be like him and I am the leader of our people now, not him. I have just witnessed the stark truth Latasha. A truth that is needed to save our kind and I will not dismiss it simply because it may be easier for me to do so or because I am too frightened to do anything about the possible futures my visions have shown me. I will not be the one known for standing back whilst our kind swirled away into extinction along with the rest of the world. Believe me when I say that my brother and my sister are still very much alive and are now fully grown and we desperately need them now, along with their Knights and their knowledge to survive in this world. Do not do me such a grave injustice by ignoring my warning girl. Without them, we will not survive. Of that I am certain."

For the first time in her life, Latasha was truly taken aback, not only by Calogero's angry attitude but also by his near admittance of disrespect for his father and his dismissal of his father's previous actions as leader of their group. Calogero, and consequently this entire situation had become about as serious as it could get. She also felt ashamed that Calogero has so blatantly pointed out a hurtful truth. She had been too uncomfortable to voice out loud what their previous leader had tried to do and more than that, she felt ashamed that she attempted to defend those actions as everyone else did if the sickening event ever surfaced in discussion.

"Shall I o...organise a search party?" she stuttered hesitantly, distinctly unsure of herself for the first time in a long while, unnerved greatly by this new Calogero in front of her. She rubbed her left thumb quickly with the fingers on her right hand in embarrassment, longing to have an excuse to escape this worsening situation even for a second.

Still disappointed in the questioning from his Knight and only real friend, Calogero stalked past her stiffly, his tail twitching from side to side displaying how she had irked him, and spoke despondently over his curved shoulder as he did so.

"If you believe in me at all Latasha, you will know that no search party is needed, and I would send no-one to perform a task that I would not be willing to undertake myself. I have seen them and I believe that I know exactly where they are, so I will go to them to retrieve them and admit wrong was done by them in order to help save our kind. It is something I should have set out to do of my own accord as soon as I became our leader but being as I cannot turn back time, I can set out no earlier than this exact moment. I will beg their forgiveness if that is what is required. You may still accompany me...if you wish to do so and if you still believe in me enough."

*****

Calogero thought deeply to himself as he padded softly through the spongy moss-covered floor of the quiet forest. Latasha walked beside him, but she was thankfully silent for the moment and he could think of nothing that he wanted to say to her since her doubtful reaction back at their home. The doubt in her green eyes and disbelieving voice had unsettled him enormously and in truth he was feeling extremely nervous and anxious already at the thought of the path that he knew he had to tread. He knew that he needed to find his siblings with intense urgency, he had witnessed the fate of the seers and the Knights without them there to offer their aid and ultimately the fate of the rest of the world, but he did not know what they would think of him seeking them out now or how they would react to this news. He had never deigned to search for them after their father had died after all. It was considered unwise at best to question the leader of the seers, especially as the leader's heir, and so he had never done so. Yet, that did not mean that he had not wanted to deny his father's demands with all his being. He had wanted to question his father when he had ordered that his new born sister be segregated from the rest of them and when he had kept his new born brother away from him too. When Calogero had heard the order of his sister's death from the whispers other seers and Knights, he had wanted to scream that it could not be true, that his father would never do such a heinous thing like that, even though deep down he had known that it was the bitter truth and that his father was capable of such a disgusting and dishonourable act. He had felt both relieved and abandoned when his mother had secretly left with the two cubs, understanding fully why she took the action that she did, but silently mourning being the one that was left behind with his unfeeling and cold-hearted father. Even though Calogero knew she would never have gotten away with taking him as well as the twins, as his father certainly would have hunted down anyway who took his heir away from him, it did not lessen the pain that he felt then and still felt to some extent now, although the pain had dulled along with his happiness over time. That was why he had vowed to himself to never get close to anyone else again unless it was absolutely essential. Even his relationship with Latasha was based more on respect and was not as friendly and carefree as those of the other seers and their Knights were. They hadn't spoken a word to each other since they had set out, even though they had been walking steadily without a pause for hours and the light had now faded to darkness. Calogero thought about mentioning stopping for the night but as Latasha hadn't mentioned it either he had decided to keep pushing on. He was concerned that he was becoming cold and unfeeling like his father but he could not seem to stop it. Even when his father had unexpectedly perished years ago, he had not felt melancholy or felt much at all in truth. The only feeling he truly harboured was disgust for himself that he had not defended his siblings at the time of his father's actions. Despite his young age and inexperience, he felt that he should have challenged his father and questioned his actions. Yet no one else had, and all had whispered that if the leader wanted it done then he must have had a good reason in a vision. No one wanted to be the one to stand out.

Letting out a brief, mournful, sigh to betray his wistfulness that things could have been different before he had the chance to suppress it, Calogero's attention was quickly caught by an unusual aroma hanging on the cool night air. He paused, blinked and sniffed the air deeply deciding that there was definitely something on the night breeze. He stopped completely and hung his mouth open to taste the air, his huge, rough, pink tongue peeking out, to catch more of the scent that he did not recognise as anything familiar.

"What is it?" whispered Latasha at the tiger's behaviour, crouching down to be nearer to Calogero's ear. "Have you scented the twins Calogero?"

The seer leader breathed in deeply again, his nostrils shrinking and then widening again as shook his head slowly in response.

"No. This scent is something different, something almost reptilian," he answered succinctly. She could see that his interest in the scent had not waned and her interruption had simply irritated him.

Latasha's brow furrowed at what she perceived as Calogero's time wasting when he was the one who had highlighted the immediacy of the danger they were in. She was annoyed that Calogero had not halted for the night as it was; although, after their disagreement, she did not want to appear to be the weaker of the two by suggesting it herself, and this needless hanging around was not doing anything to improve her current irritated temperament. Her arms crossed tightly across her chest as she rose to her feet.

"Ignore it then. We are looking for seers and Knights. Not measly reptiles," she spat impatiently.

A singsong voice that was not Calogero's, chimed out into the night in answer to her unkind utterance.

"Well, luckily for you, the Decona could not be further from measly reptiles, but a proud race that have recently become acquainted with your kind once again and may have need of some of you."

Latasha snarled aggressively, even going as far as to show her rounded, white, teeth. She had developed tiger like instincts after being with Calogero and the other seers for so long and used them instinctively, without preamble. Her hand slid to the scabbard buckled to her side, and clutched at the jewelled handle of the broadsword encased there. Calogero's fur on the back of his neck and his shoulders had also risen into prickly rivets and his long tail had puffed out making him appear larger than he was, as his emerald green eyes surveyed the three lizard like beings that had just intentionally come into their view.

"You would think to attack us, the Decona?" sang the incredulous voice, which just happened to belong to Shesha Decona, "You have not nearly as much foresight or grace as Loki Soothsayer. Bring him to me at once. I have questions that I would ask of him."

Calogero discarded his wariness immediately at the mention of Loki's name.

"Who are you and what do you know of Loki?" bellowed Calogero rudely, still backed by a snarling Latasha.

Without replying, Shesha pulled a wicked looking throwing blade from a metal strap looped around her leg and launched it. It missed Latasha by an inch and embedded itself with a loud thunk into the Unfortunate that had appeared beside her. Calogero's and Latasha's gaze swung to the creature instantly.

The creature cackled madly and pulled the circular blade from its shoulder with no hint of pain and flicked it to the ground with distain as two more beings, similar to it in appearance glided out of the darkness and flanked the group, laughing as they did so.

"Stay away from them Latasha," ordered Calogero sternly, backing away as he did. "These are the creatures from my vision. I cannot kill them!"

An immense crackling fireball whooshed past the tiger as he

issued his orders. It came from the direction that Shesha and the two Decona had emerged from and hit the Unfortunate that Shesha had attacked with full force. The Unfortunate burst into flames, flakes of ash circled up into the air around him as he clawed at himself uselessly.

"But I can," Everhart announced as he calmly strolled into the melee. Athena danced merrily by his side, protecting Everhart's parents, Freya and Loki who walked behind her with thick weaves of air. They were however, unrequired, as on seeing Everhart and his green eyes, the remaining two creatures sped off hastily in order to report to their Master.

"Ah, excellent timing Loki. I have been looking for you and your Everhart" sang Shesha with a slight bow. "I have a few things that I should like to discuss with you at your earliest convenience."

"As do I brother," boomed Calogero.

31

    Loki and Everhart were certain that if their hearts or minds were assaulted with any more surprises then they would crumble. The events and occurrences of the past few months had left their heads whirling, yet they had no time to slow down and absorb the new found knowledge fully, for there were horrifying dangers that were a real threat lurking in the darkness that could not simply be ignored in the hope that they would go away. Calogero, who had shockingly turned out to be Loki's elder brother and sole leader of the remaining seers started the confusing explanations, but implored them to let him be as brief as possible for the time being, for he had experienced the visions of the Unfortunates too and sensed that time was of the essence if they were to defend those they loved against this menace. He detailed these to Everhart and Loki, adding that his visions had hinted that the two of them were absolutely paramount to the demise of the vile beasts that he could not kill himself. Shesha Decona was quite perturbed that Calogero had possessed the audacity to put his requests forward prior to her own, but Loki, in his effortless sympathetic manner had calmed her and begged her to still speak her important tale and when she was done, Everhart cleared his throat to put some of the pieces of the puzzle into place so the bigger picture could be viewed by all.

    "I actually think that I can help you unravel some of the

mysteries here Lady Shesha," he began confidently, "for after we had been parted from your company and were blessed in making a new friend, we were savagely and cruelly attacked without warning. At first, I thought that it had been one of your own Decona that had tackled us, for the creature looked vaguely akin to your kind, with silvery scales and deadly claws. The beast cruelly murdered our friend Vita, who was only there at all for the sakes of Loki and I. We were and still are absolutely devastated at the loss, as I am certain you were at the loss of one of your own. I could not understand why your people would do such a thing to us after you had gifted us with such marvellous weapons and aided us kindly on our way. However, when I started to become furious with delusions of revenge and seething anger, our new-found friend and ally Mopsus corrected my erroneous assumptions. He was under the impression that the attacker was in fact, a bitter twisted man named Willian from our own distant village of Aither who had followed us in the hope of gaining some great power from Loki. Mopsus suggested that he had drunk of the blood of a Decona, he had probably heard the legends of your blood granting memories from generation to generation, but the blood twisted him in a vile and unnatural manner, because it was never meant for him to consume. So, truly, it was my fault that one of your children perished well before their time, for it was I that Willian detested enough to go to these extremes. I was the one that he followed. I was the one who led him to your door."

After his speech, Everhart knelt silently on one knee on the ground in front of Shesha and her two companions and bowed his head, exposing the skin on the back of his neck.

Loki, looking aghast, quickly padded to the side of his friend and included both Shesha and Everhart in his gaze as he spoke.

"That is not the truth and we all know it. It was I that the wretched Willian wanted, thinking I could grant him all sorts of impossible powers and glory. If anyone should be held responsible and punished for this, it should be me."

Loki and Everhart's newly constructed family gulped in unison, whilst Everhart's mother pulled Athena close to her automatically. Everhart opened his mouth to contradict his faithful friend, but before he uttered a word Calogero boomed out impatiently.

"No-one will be punishing either of you if I have anything to do with it and I assure you that I shall. We need you. The world needs you to end this threat. And I know the one you speak of, Mopsus, from my days as a cub. If he said that this is what happened then I will believe that no-one is responsible for the unfortunate death of the Decona than this twisted human. No-one but himself made the damaging decisions to behave as he did and accepting his failures as anything but his own is ridiculous."

He narrowed his feline eyes at Shesha, testing her to disagree with him, but surprisingly she let out a chiming laugh and hauled

Everhart to his feet by his well-muscled arm.

"I think you need my help big man and perhaps I shall indeed punish you if you fail to accept it. Tell us what you know about these creatures and how it is that this temperamental tiger here thinks that you are the ones that can save us from them."

An almost collective sigh of relief issued forth from the gathering, as they felt the dissipation of the brewing altercation that now appeared to have been avoided.

Everhart grinned a tight smile and nodded curtly at Lady Shesha. Still keeping eye contact with her so that he could absorb her reaction, he raised his right palm in the air and ignited a small patch of twirling, scarlet fire within it. Luckily, he failed to see Latasha roll her eyes and cross her arms as he demonstrated his Knight's skills.

"So far, in our experiences with the Unfortunates, as Loki was told they were called in a vision, this is the only thing that has stopped them. Loki was flung aside as easily as a rag doll when he attacked them tooth and claw. Ripping them apart is apparently not the answer. I think that the only way we will be able to defeat them is to use Knight's fire to burn them to ash. However, they are incredibly agile and faster than we could ever hope to be, as you have just witnessed. On our last run in with them they were also in a group of three, which obviously increases the issue three-fold. I simply wasn't quick enough to take out all three of them at once then or now, so we will need as many Knights as you have to contend with the possibility of large numbers. Unfortunately, I do not know how many of these creatures there are in total, so I think it would be prudent to err on the side of caution and to amass as large an army as we can. Calogero, how many of your people would be willing to fight with us if it came to that?"

Calogero drew in a deep breath.

"If I decree it, then all of my seer's Knights will fight without question, but there are little more than forty of us including seers and some of us are old now, we do not have the luxury of youth on our side."

Everhart gritted his teeth together resolutely and fought to keep the dismay from his neutral expression.

"It will have to do!"

Unbeknown to the makeshift war committee, the two remaining Unfortunates had not retreated as far as they would have liked, although they had backed off a goodly enough distance that they would not be seen by any of the gathering. As Unfortunates, they had the benefit of miraculous hearing and consequently, they had picked up on everything that the group had discussed. On hearing the total number of foes opposed to them, they sped off truly this time, in order to report this new information to the Original.

32

When only two of the scouting party returned to report, instead of the initial three that were sent out, the Original was beyond furious and had mercilessly beaten the two who had returned until he had calmed down enough to speak. Whilst he did so, his burly right hand man stood stock still by his side; large arms folded neatly and simply watched the proceedings in front of him, without even blinking an eye, let alone mouthing any word of objection to the brutal beating.

"The reason that I wanted you to report to me immediately," hissed The Original through gritted teeth, "was due to the fact that I did not wish you to be seen, thus, providing us with the element of surprise so we could decimate them without warning as quickly as possible. You are fortunate that you brought me information of their numbers, or else I would have been really angry. Having made another ten of you, I anticipate that figure not being too much of a hassle to us. Now go and round up the others you idiots, I want us organised and ready to leave by this time tomorrow. You pair will lead us to them."

The two skittered away, low down on their stomachs, like dogs that had just been reprimanded, as soon as they were able to. The Original sneered after them, disgusted at their lack of competency and sickening idiocy. He obviously would need his burly right hand to instil into the group that when he issued an order, it was to be followed to the letter regardless of any intermittent factors. If not, there would be severe repercussions. The Original had wanted to test out a theory that as he created the beings himself, he would be able to terminate their lives as well. Possessing more ingenuity and intelligence than the others seemed to have, however he decided to leave this little experiment until after he had dealt with this green-eyed pest problem. That would give him something to look forward too after this brief foray.

The burly Unfortunate cleared his throat gently to draw the Original's attention back from his private thoughts.

"Do you have any orders Master?" he asked mundanely.

The Original eyed him thoughtfully, a slender index finger delicately holding his chin whilst his thumb propped itself under his jaw.

"Yes. Organise these wasteful wretches into coherent forces and ensure that when we launch our attack, they focus all their energy on the green-eyed humans and ignore the tigers, leaving them until last when we can terminate them at a leisurely pace being as they are of little threat to us. Emphasise that I do not want them attacking the humans individually. Impose on them the importance of teaming up to launch an aggressive attack. That will give us the advantage, as from what I hear, they aren't blessed with superior speed as we are. And let them know, if my orders are not followed exactly, I will be most displeased and I will visit that displeasure down among them slowly as an example to the rest of our group."

The right-hand Unfortunate did not need to be told more than once and he flitted away immediately to inform the coven of their duties. He would follow his orders as instructed and ensure that if any punishment was meted out, he would not be on the receiving end of it.

33

Calogero, with Latasha at his side, had eagerly led their new recruits back to the home of the seers and the Knights and had wasted no time in calling an immediate gathering to discuss the grave and impending problem that had arisen. If Loki and Everhart had expected the home of their ancestors to be some welcoming, magical, enchanting city akin to that of the home of the Decona's dwelling, then they were sorely mistaken. There were no towering architectural wonders to be awed at here. In fact, the only structures that had been constructed looked vaguely permanent at best. Small wooden shacks stood awkwardly and haphazardly amongst the clearing, their only distinguishable feature were the wide doorways big enough to admit a large tiger with comfort and ease. These appeared to be the only housing that was available. There was one structure that was marginally larger than the rest, although its frame was still constructed of ordinary timber, it possessed a well-kept flagstone floor and Latasha had quietly informed him that this was the 'great' hall in which any meetings of importance were held.

In fact, Everhart thought that this place had no sense of 'home' to it whatsoever. It felt to him, as if the seers and the Knights that had set out to distance themselves from humans could just physically travel no further and had simply stopped here and given up. It was almost as if this place was built with the intention of being temporary, but hope had vanished and the willingness to build something beautiful had never re-emerged. The sight of the unloved settlement filled Everhart's heavy heart with true sorrow and the suspicion that he was missing another problem here, although more imminent issues were at the forefront of his mind at the present moment in time. A glance at Loki's dejected eyes assured Everhart that he felt the same way but evidently he had found no way to fix this as yet. This group felt damaged and destitute. It was not to be entirely unexpected however. On the walk back here, Calogero had talked a lot about the past, present and future of their people, and had apologised with downcast eyes at the actions of his father and for not searching for his siblings when he had had the chance after he had perished. This decision seemed to have had a huge, negative impact on the seers and the Knights, despite the fact that, thankfully, the once leader of the seer's true wishes had not been successful in being carried out. Loki had wanted to interject to forgive his brother but Everhart had shaken his head and whispered to Loki to allow the seer leader to say what he felt he needed to say. This was obviously a burden that he had carried for many years and would not be easily cleared. They could talk when they were gathered in front of everybody. And that was where they found themselves now. Calogero had just briefed those gathered on the stark seriousness of the situation and who was who among their new guests, and had now courteously invited Everhart and Loki to speak.

Everhart nervously cleared his throat and stepped forward with Loki at his side. "I think that your leader has already detailed what is needed now. In the main, we need everyone that there is to fight against this evil. Lady Shesha has courageously offered to stand with us also. Unfortunately, she does not have time to summon the rest of her people before we feel we need to act, but she will do her utmost to protect us whilst we fight with fire against the Unfortunates."

"Protect us?!" asked an elderly voice disbelieving, "allow me to introduce myself young Everhart, I am Sandro, and whilst I would never shirk my responsibility to my people, as you can clearly see, I am not as sprightly as I once was, and neither is my bonded seer here. If these creatures cannot be defeated with anything other than our fire, how am I to protect my seer whilst wielding it against them? And with all due respect Lady Shesha, I doubt that you can do any better at deflecting these near invincible creatures with the martial abilities you possess if our fire is all that can stop them."

Lady Shesha held her chin up defiantly.

"The more eyes we have, the better chance we will have at helping you Knight's to locate and destroy these beasts. I will not hesitate to aid in this way if that is all that I can do," she sang.

"I do not doubt your courage," Sandro retorted, "but I doubt your courage will stop you or my seer from perishing when the attention of the Knights is diverted elsewhere."

A silence, which was louder and more deafening than any noise descended on the room. Everyone gathered recognised the bitter truth of these words. The horrendous silence was broken with a delighted giggle.

Athena skipped up to Everhart and Loki, tapped them each upon the shoulder and danced a circle around the pair excitedly. Sandro, outraged, was quickly hushed by Calogero before he could create uproar, the leader having realised Athena's temperament was not like anyone else that he had met from re-encountering her and remembering how she was when she was born.

"These ones aren't really mean like the ones that mother ran us away from Ever," she giggled smiling, "they are just a bit scared, that's all. I used to be scared once but I'm not now. I will help them like I helped your parents when we were attacked before. I've fixed it so they can have little ones again too brother. They don't need to be sad anymore, the children will make them happy again."

The mutterings that broke out could no longer be quelled.

34

The night was eerily silent and awash with anticipation. The Knight's and the seers had discussed tactics as much as they could, debating whether to have the Knight's leave their home and have the seers remain with any non-magically gifted humans, protected by the three Decona headed by Lady Shesha, or whether to fight their cause as a group altogether at their home. Everhart had formed a mini war council along with Calogero, Loki, Latasha, Shesha and Freya and Athena. His parents had also been present at the council, not wanting to leave Athena without them on such a serious and significant gathering. Calogero had raised his concern sternly that if the Knights were to leave, then there was no sure way of knowing whether this would cause more harm than good ultimately, as if The Unfortunates split their forces and launched an attack at home with no Knight's at all present to act in defence, then those that had remained would stand absolutely no chance against the might, strength and speed of the monstrous creatures. Everhart had suggested splitting the Knights instead so that some would remain at home, although he conceded despairingly that this would create more of a risk for the main force, leaving them at a severe disadvantage as their numbers were significantly less than ideal as they were. Loki had hopefully conveyed his opinion that perhaps the whole group could leave the home site together and set off to a more advantageous fighting ground for them. He pointed out that although it was not much, at least if they selected his option, it may provide their home with a greater chance of surviving the inevitable carnage that would surely follow this clash. Freya had irritably disagreed, stating that she would detest being a liability to Athena and the other Knights around her as they struggled to fight and defend all at once. In response to this Athena had buried her face deeply into the tiger's striped fur and hugged her tightly, her slender hands gripping fistfuls of fur.

"But I'm supposed to look after you Freya, I'm your Knight and anyway, I might be able to fit the rest in with you if I try hard enough, well some of them anyway. I tried to say before but everybody was getting flustered."

Freya's eyes grew watery, she was no seer, but her truest friend still thought that she was worth protecting. However, Freya was left no time for this emotional moment.

"What does she mean?" Latasha had interjected rudely, purposefully not addressing Athena directly. She had already made her distaste known that Athena had been included on the war council, but when Calogero had sided with his siblings over her after they had strenuously objected to her being omitted, Latasha had been left with no choice but to begrudgingly accede to the decision.

Everhart's mother tutted in a disappointed manner at the

harsh tone Latasha used.

"Our Athena has the ability to create an incredibly strong shield, from air so Everhart has led me to believe, which she has already utilised with great success in the past to protect us and keep us safe from these Unfortunates." The pride in her voice was unmistakeable.

Everhart continued the speech for her.

"As Mopsus pointed out to me during our time together, it seems that all Knights have their individual strengths. Whilst mine is fire, Athena's is the manipulation of wind and air. She can create a far stronger shield than I could ever hope to and I daresay more powerful than the majority of, if not all, of the Knight's living here. Although she seems unable to command the other elements, her strength in air is unparalleled. The shield that she created during our previous encounter with the Unfortunates was absolutely impenetrable."

"I just don't know how big I can make it go," she whispered in a concerned tone, "but I will do my best so that as few of us as possible get hurt."

Everhart's parents hugged her tightly.

35

The moon was full and heavy in the twinkling twilight sky. No drifting clouds masked its looming presence and it oozed that eerie feeling that something was watching you and that predators were on the prowl, when the hairs on the back of your neck stand up on edge unbidden, thought Everhart to himself, rubbing his neck subconsciously. He had taken charge of the makeshift army with Calogero's encouragement and blessing and was now stood at the head of the gathering. They had egressed from the permanent home of the seers and the Knights after much discussion and debate, to a huge clearing a few miles off. No-one had been left behind. Athena stood at the very centre of the gathering, with members of the group that had been deemed to be more vulnerable, such as Everhart's parents and other non-Knight humans. She held the hands of her adoptive parents protectively and her eyes were lidded. The seers had stoically refused to leave the sides of their twinned Knights, so the tiger and human peers were ringed neatly around this core forming a protective crust, with Shesha and her two Decona flanking Everhart and Loki. Athena had attempted to throw her air shield out over the group before battle began, but it wavered and would not hold securely.

"When she feels we are threatened she will be able to hold it over us," Freya had assured them confidently, "Athena has ever worked on emotion, and her magic usually is at its strongest when we need it the most."

Everhart and Loki had not disagreed. They had witnessed this for themselves and would not let Athena think that they doubted her. Everhart had shrugged it off anyway as if it did not work, they still were left with no choice but to fight regardless, so it would simply mean that they would have to fight all the harder to prevent casualties and protect their people.

Loki began whimpering at Everhart's side. The Knight looked down to see his friend's eyes had rolled back into his head and his mouth was twitching uncomfortably and uncontrollably. Everhart laid a reassuring hand on the tiger's back and waited patiently as he felt the steady rise and fall of Loki's breath. Eventually his companion came back to the realms of reality. He immediately looked up to Everhart and mouthed painfully,

"Be ready. They are coming now, in full force. To stop the rot only the destruction of the leader will be sufficient, for he alone has the power to breathe a new life close to death into those that he chooses."

Everhart relayed the message back and lit a Knight's fire within his cupped hands. The darkness in front of him was illuminated, revealing the oncoming onslaught of terror.

"FIRE!" bellowed Everhart as loudly as he could.

The first fire volley caused the silence of the night to be

obliterated by the death screeches of those Unfortunate that were first hit by the catapulting magic. Nevertheless, Everhart was more than aware that the battle was not going to be won so easily as this.

The flashes of light illuminated in the darkness, the ear-splitting noise and the sickly charred stench all conspired together to conjure up a terrifying and confusing atmosphere to fight in. Just as Everhart raised his arm to blast another fiery shot out in the oncoming onslaught, he heard a surprised and startled grunt from his side. Loki had been seized by a crazed Unfortunate and mercilessly flung over the beast's shoulder. It did not appear that Loki was the creature's true target and nothing but a hindrance, but the adrenaline was already pumping through Everhart's veins and his fear for Loki left no time to be calm or for rational thought. Everhart leapt after his faithful friend and rolled onto the cold, hard, earth towards him. Only when the ravaging claws ripped mercilessly through the thick muscle on his left shoulder did Everhart fathom that he was now certainly beyond the safety of Athena's protective shield. The white hot pain blossoming out through his screeching shoulder and down into his elbow seemed to be having a negative impact on his magical ability. Attempting to construct a fireball simply seemed to produce a brief spark and the gagging stench of a recently doused fire.

Everything seemed to move in slow motion for a moment. Everhart could see a battered and bruised Loki rearing up behind the night-time menace that loomed above him, his own blood still dripping from its outstretched talons, the creature that Loki had no possible hope of defeating or overpowering now that his magic was lost to him.

Everhart had hesitated once before, to the detriment of his friend Vita, who had paid the dearest cost, with her own life. He refused to hesitate again, magic or no magic. With a great roar, Everhart leapt nimbly from the ground and unsheathed his deadly blade from its scabbard, swinging it with no heed for the pain in his torn shoulder. The blade sliced neatly with ease through the exposed neck of the Unfortunate and the creature's head thudded audibly to the ground amidst spurts of rank blood and gore, moments before its carcass joined it there in a twisted heap. Loki landed on all four paws atop of the gruesome mess.

"Everhart, are you alright?" breathlessly rasped out Loki, wincing at the blood that was still leaking from him, "Look at your arm...and your sword!"

The Knight ignored the searing pain in his arm with some effort and glanced at the sword in his clenched fist. It was glowing softly with a deep scarlet hue, akin to that of dying embers, although it did not feel hot to the touch for Everhart. It appeared that when he had not been able to muster the strength to conjure a fireball between his bare hands to attack with, he had instead somehow channelled his energy and magic into his sword instead, which proved to be just as effective at putting the Unfortunate's down although obviously this method of attack was more risky due to the close fighting quarters required. Everhart was not sure how he had managed it, but right now he truly did not have the time to consider it thoroughly and just settled for being grateful. Loki was already digging his sharp teeth into Everhart's soft collar and dragging him laboriously back to the safety of Athena's shield, which she now seemed to have been able to emanate over their group. A silvery sheen hung over the majority of their friend and kin, although a few arms, shoulders and tails did jut out here and there. Everhart scrambled to his feet, freeing Loki's grasp and clutched the tiger instead as the two of them headed towards the haven of light beckoning them towards it. Seconds from reaching it, two figures seemed to appear before them from nowhere. Everhart examined them, dragging his eyes from their feet right up to their faces. When his eyes settled there he could not help but let out a startled gasp.

36

Barley Wheatflour, devoid of any hint of emotion, stared back at Everhart with abysmal, blank, black eyes. Barley had his still flabby mouth slightly ajar and two white, curved fangs were evident, set perfectly in the top row of his otherwise rounded teeth. Everhart realised with a deep pang of regret, that surprised him, that Barley, the rough handed baker that his parents had paid to take him in when they set out on their journey, no longer existed as he had once known him and had truly become an Unfortunate.

"Barley? Barley Wheatflour? What are you doing? Don't you know who you are? Don't you know me?" questioned Everhart in a desperate, pleading voice, his trembling hand wavering a small distance from the baker's rotund frame, unable to quite bring himself to touch the person that he had once known and once fervently hated.

"It appears that this human thinks that he knows you, Unfortunate," creaked the other figure's voice with a hint of sadistic amusement.

Everhart dragged his gaze reluctantly away from his old guardian to stare at the speaker with the sarcastic, creaky voice. He too possessed eyes as dark as black, freshly-dug graves and just as deep, although his hair was long, sleek and deathly white and a strong confidence exuded from him like the scent of the strongest perfume imaginable, marking him unmistakably as the leader of these ravenous and hellish creatures. Loki's words at the beginning of this fateful night echoed through his head monumentally and he silently vowed that he would not lose sight of this creature and risk more of his kind being brought into existence to wreak havoc among the world that he cherished. He was aware that death would either find him or them tonight and he was damn sure it was not going to be him that perished. His dead-looking lips curved slightly upwards, creasing his hollow cheek in a sadistic smirk indicating his amusement at the horrific situation that they were currently mired in. After staring at the masochistic beast for what felt like an eternity of seconds, Everhart realised that he actually recognised the wan face that callously grinned back at him as well.

"I am sure that I do not know this human, Master," replied Barley in an unsure voice that wavered slightly at the end of the sentence he uttered, "I only know you and the life of the Unfortunates. I am at your service as always Creator."

"Master? Creator?" queried Everhart, his suspicions that this confrontation was definitely with the leader of the group that now plagued their kind, now confirmed undeniably, "I know who you are now, pale one. However, last time that I saw you, you were master of nothing and no-one. You were just that poor, pathetic wretch that used to bounce around the heels of the treacherous Willian Liew. All the people of Aither said that you were dumb and most felt sorry for you; you were too pathetic to be despised or hated. If only they could see you now!"

The Original spat angrily at Everhart, a very human thing to do thought the Knight.

"Yes, I wish that they could all see me and the power that I have attained now! You know nothing of what I am now, you green-eyed fool! I am your true doom and always was, just as I was the doom of that dusty, pathetic village that you once resided in - the one that we tore asunder! You see, I remember you as well, I hunted you with another and I have now decided that the hunt has not ceased yet. You will die." The Original hoped to unnerve his opponent with the mention of the ransacked previous home that he had once had, but Everhart was determined to remain focused and conceal any sorrow from the eyes of those that he faced.

This time Everhart smirked, although it was not as gleeful as the Original's twisted, horrific grin. Everhart's smile was nonchalant on the outside, but anyone that knew him would realise that it was a farce and tainted with sorrow.

"Well, I have to let you know that didn't work out too well for your friend Willian, and I guess that you are going to have to discover that we won't give in to tyranny and bullying the same way that Willian found out!"

Without hesitation, Everhart roared a battle cry and swung his gleaming sword in a huge arc above his head with his good arm.

The formidable weapon was now resonating with the pure power of ferocious flames and consequently it slid with ease through the scrawny neck of the leader and through the thick shoulder and collarbone of Barley Wheatflour. Everhart would rather not have harmed Barley if it could have been helped, despite the disdainful way he had been treated at his hands, for he had grown from childhood to manhood whilst living under his roof in the now decimated Aither. However, he knew of no way that this tragic transformation could be reversed and he was sure that Barley had already perished long before this encounter. Before thick blood could manage to surge from the gaping, open wounds of the two Unfortunates who had fallen under the Knight's sword, they erupted into two flailing figures of flame before disintegrating into mounds of warm, soft, grey, ash. The leader of the Unfortunates was dead. Everhart was not sure what he had thought would happen when this moment arrived, whether he had imagined the rest of the Unfortunate's would fall to the ground dead immediately at the death of their maker or whether they would automatically surrender when his life was snuffed out, but the reality of the situation was that nothing changed and the situation was just as dire as it had previously been. The fraught fighting continued around Loki and himself. The choking stench of charred flesh clung determinedly to the insides of his nostrils making his throat feel greasy and his stomach sicken whilst his nostrils attempted to shrink to reduce the rancid onslaught. Despite this, he had to carry on and ensure those fighting with him were protected from these twisted creatures.

For hours and hours, bloody, black, claws slashed at the bright barrier as it held sturdily, burning fires blazed and violence reigned through the early hours of the darkness. Eventually, when the night had fled to make way for the morning, the battle was over and the post-war battlefield was the most peculiar battlefield site that Everhart could have ever imagined. The sun was just lazily climbing up into the morning sky, but the fresh morning breeze was marred by the rancid odour of cremated meat and of damp, sodden, ash. Mounds of the powdery, grey, ash littered the earth where bloodied corpses would usually lie after a hard battle and sprinklings of ash danced gracefully on the currents of the morning breeze.

Dried, flaky, blood had crusted over Everhart's shoulder and in rivulets down his muscly arm, wrist and through his fingers. He would need to get his throbbing injury seen too when he could, but thankfully his wound appeared to the be the worst one that had been inflicted on their side, thanks to the magnificent might of Athena's shimmering shield. Everyone was emphatically exhausted but miraculously, not a single one of the party had been maimed, seriously injured or killed and if Loki's visions rang true, now that the white-haired Unfortunate was deceased, no more of his foul kind could be produced. Calogero thanked his people solemnly and promised a speech when they got back home after some much needed rest and recuperation.

The seers and the Knights headed back home together, followed by the three Decona, ready to build their new future.

Printed in Great Britain
by Amazon